NO SHAME, NO FEAR

NO SHAME,
NO FEAR

ANN TURNBULL

CANDLEWICK PRESS
CAMBRIDGE, MASSACHUSETTS

I should like to thank Ted Milligan
for reading the manuscript and advising
me on Quaker history.

Copyright © 2003 by Ann Turnbull

First U.S. paperback edition 2006

The Library of Congress has cataloged the hardcover edition as follows:
Turnbull, Ann.
No shame, no fear / Ann Turnbull. — 1st U.S. ed.
p. cm.
Summary: In England in 1662, a time of religious persecution,
fifteen-year-old Susanna, a poor country girl and a Quaker, and
seventeen-year-old William, a wealthy Anglican,
meet and fall in love against all odds.
ISBN-10 0-7636-2505-1 (hardcover)
ISBN-13 978-0-7636-2505-4 (hardcover)
[1. Religious persecution — Fiction. 2. Quakers — Fiction.
3. Social classes — Fiction. 4. Great Britain — History — Charles II,
1660–1685 — Fiction.] I. Title.
PZ7.T8493No 2004
[Fic] — dc22   2003065280

ISBN-10 0-7636-3190-6 (paperback)
ISBN-13 978-0-7636-3190-1 (paperback)

2 4 6 8 10 9 7 5 3 1

Printed in the United States of America

This book was typeset in Cochin and Aqualine.

Candlewick Press
2067 Massachusetts Avenue
Cambridge, Massachusetts 02140

visit us at www.candlewick.com

To Tim, David, and Julie,
whose encouragement and enthusiasm
kept me going

SHROPSHIRE
1662

Susanna

We were having a washday when the bailiffs came. We'd gotten the linen together, piled in a basket — shirts, shifts, caps, sheets, collars: a fortnight's load — and I was helping my mother lay it in the tub, spreading it out and placing sticks between the layers so that water could soak through evenly.

The tub was in the hall, and although it was cold outside, we'd left the house door open to let out the smell and steam. There was a deal of noise, water splashing and the clang of pails on flagstones, and we'd been at it since dawn. Our sleeves were rolled up, and I knew my face must be as pink as my mother's, for it was heavy work.

Isaac and Deb were in the yard at the side of the house. He was chopping firewood, and she was feeding the hens. They appeared suddenly in the doorway, their faces sharp with alarm.

"They're at the top of the lane!" said Isaac. "With a cart!"

Deb had her thumb in her mouth. I went to the door and she ran to me and butted her head against my skirt. I lifted her up. I knew she was frightened. My own heart was racing.

"They won't hurt thee, chicken," I said.

Deb spoke around her thumb. "Not a chicken."

We'd known they were coming, of course. That was why my mother had chosen that day as washday. We won't hinder the law, but we know how to be awkward. The big buck-tub was in the middle of the hall, leaving room for people to pass, but not for furniture.

I saw a knot of neighbors in the lane, glancing between us and the approaching men. There was an eagerness about them. Not much happens in Long Aston.

Any other family, and they might have offered support: fists shaken at the bailiffs, maybe even a barricade. But not us. Even so, when I'd gone the day before to fetch beer from the inn, the landlord had said, almost in irritation, "Hide some valuables, girl. And put a few chickens in a crate and bring them here. We'll keep them till they've gone."

It was the first kindness he'd shown us. He felt pity, I realized, now that my father was in prison and my mother had no one to protect her.

But I could only thank him and answer, "It's not our way."

He clicked his teeth then, and said, "No. Your way is to make martyrs of yourselves. But folk don't think any better of you for it."

Now the bailiffs were at the gate. They dismounted with a clatter of weapons and harnesses, and strode up to the door. My mother had just tipped a pailful of ley into the tub, and the smell rose up: wood ash, and the urine that we put in to bleach the linen. She faced the bailiffs while I took the younger ones indoors. I set Deb down and told her and Isaac to go up to the loft. But Isaac wouldn't go, and Deb stayed close by his side.

"Elizabeth Thorn?"

There were three of them, tall in their high-crowned black hats. The leader produced a warrant.

"Elizabeth Thorn, your husband stands convicted of nonpayment of church tithes, being one-tenth of all your income, and in default of payment I am empowered to distrain upon your goods."

My mother stepped back into the hall, and then into the parlor, and we had the small satisfaction of watching them squeeze, one by one, past the buck-tub. But, once inside, they seemed to fill the house with their male presence: loud voices, boots, weapons.

The leader began making an inventory. The others pulled at the bed, tossed pillows and blankets on the floor. They flung out the contents of our oak chest: linen cloths and sheets, spare clothes, my father's leather jerkin, my mother's black hat that she wears to market. One of them was sent outside, and soon we heard the hens screeching and squawking. Good girls, I thought: You give him the runaround.

They tramped around our small kitchen, finding little of value. In the parlor the leader noted my father's loom, which stood against the wall opposite the bed.

He made a decision. "Take the bed and the loom."

I know my mother had intended to stay quiet. But she is a fiery woman, and when she saw them begin to drag out the bed she shared with my father, she said, "We will pay no tithes to any hireling priest! The Word of God is free. Did Christ demand tithes? Did he—"

"Be quiet, woman, or you will find yourself in worse trouble," the leader said.

And they took the bed that had been hers since her marriage. When they reached the hall, one of them heaved at the buck-tub and pushed it over, sending scalding water flowing across the floor. I leaped aside just in time, but I yelped in fright. Deb began to scream.

With the bed stowed on the cart, they came back for the loom, which had a length of cloth on it.

"The yarn is not ours," my mother said quickly. "My husband works to order."

They cut the cloth free and tossed it down on the basket of yarn. Then they started to carry out the loom.

My mother ran after them. "How is my husband to work?" she demanded.

But they ignored her. And we saw that the one who had been in the yard had crated up the chickens and was bringing out Pleasance, our cow.

In the lane a small group of people watched and gossiped as the cart was driven off with a man walking behind it leading the cow. Two girls I knew a little stared at me and whispered behind their hands. I looked away, lifting my chin. I was lonely at Long Aston, and had never found friends among the village girls. No doubt their parents warned them against me. Our family was different. My father didn't drink with the men at the alehouses; my mother didn't gossip; in defiance of the law, we never went to that steeple-house they called their church, and neither was my father willing to pay tithes to its priest. And for this our neighbors saw us punished and perhaps thought we deserved it.

"Help me with the tub, Su," my mother said.

Together we hauled it upright, gathered up the hot, waterlogged linen, dirty now from the floor, and relaid it in the tub. My mother mopped the floor. Isaac took Deb out to the yard, and I walked into the parlor and saw the empty spaces where the bed and the loom had been, the blankets and pillows and other things scattered around. I began to tidy up.

When we'd set the house aright it looked emptier than ever. Then Isaac came running in and released two hens into the room.

"They missed these!"

Deb squealed and chased them. And somehow we all caught her excitement and laughed like daft things over the escape of those two hens.

"Well," my mother said, "we have hens; there is straw in the loft to sleep on; and they have left me my spinning wheel."

But they'd taken our cow. That was a great loss. I put on my pattens and went outside to check the cowshed and outhouses. The door of the cowshed was open. Inside, I smelled the warm reek of manure and the scent of hay. It was as if Pleasance was still there, and I half expected to hear her bumping against the woodwork of her stall, eager to be milked.

My eyes pricked with tears, and I felt a surge of resentment toward my parents for their stubborn faith, which had brought us to this. And then at once I felt guilty, for it was my faith, too; I was the eldest child and must help my family — and as I thought about this, I saw that at the same time I might be able to change my own life for the better.

I said nothing until the evening. We prayed together and ate supper, and Deb went to her bed in the loft. Isaac took up the Bible, as my father would do of an evening, and read aloud from Luke's gospel. When Isaac, too, had gone to bed, my mother and I sat together by rushlight and the embers of the fire, my mother spinning while I knitted a stocking. Our shadows moved on the walls, and the wheel made a gentle clicking background to my thoughts.

"Mam," I said, "we can't live by spinning. I've turned fifteen. I must leave home and find work."

I made it sound like a duty, but the truth is I was eager to go: to a town, a place where folk were not so superstitious, so set in their ways, a place where I wouldn't always be an outsider but would meet others with beliefs like ours, other girls — and perhaps boys.

I saw from her face that she realized the sense of it.

"But who would take thee, hereabouts?"

I knew she was remembering the time last year when I'd worked for a few months helping the dairymaid on a neighbor's farm. Two of the cows had fallen sick and the maid had pointed the finger at me; said she'd seen me making signs over them. All lies, and fool's talk, too, for my father says there is no such thing as witchcraft, only the darkness of folks' minds. But they looked askance at me, and I was afraid; it was lucky for me the cows recovered.

"Thou must go to Friends of Truth," my mother decided. "Perhaps Alice Randall needs a dairymaid."

Alice is a widow with a farm out at Crowbank, miles from anywhere.

"Not a farm," I said. "I want to go to town. To Hemsbury."

"The town?" Her face showed anxiety. My mother has traveled, but she is a countrywoman at heart. She thinks towns are full of ungodliness.

"It's not far," I said, "and there are Friends there. Many more than around here. Shopkeepers and suchlike, who might need servants. And some who might have daughters my age."

She looked at me then as if she had at last understood.

"Yes," she said. "Thou needst young company. And if we could find thee a place with godly folk . . ."

"We could ask after Meeting," I said.

I had thought it all out.

❊   ❊   ❊

And so, on first-day, as the bell was clanging to call folk to the steeple-house, we set off as usual to walk the seven miles across country to the meeting at Eaton Bellamy.

It's rough walking there, along lanes deep in mud, over stiles and ditches, but we're used to it — even little Deb; she trudged along, holding her doll, Sibley, who keeps her amused during the long meetings. We passed few travelers till we reached the outskirts of Eaton Bellamy. There we saw some folk on horseback riding toward us: a merchant, I guessed — a middle-aged man with several packhorses and servants behind — and with him a young man who sat tall in the saddle and wore a fine black hat with a gray plume in it.

We had to cross the road in front of them to reach a stile on the other side. We were almost across when Deb cried out that she had dropped Sibley's hood. She darted back, stumbled over a rut, and fell, letting out one of her piercing wails. The merchant's horse shied. He swore and struggled to control it, and the party halted.

I ran to help Deb, but the young man had already dismounted and reached her just ahead of me. He lifted her to her feet. Deb looked up, saw a stranger's face, and the wail stopped in her throat. She stared, wide-eyed, then flew to my arms.

The young man looked at me and smiled. I liked

his smile, and the way he had cared about Deb; for he was clearly a well-to-do youth, and many such would have cursed us and ridden on.

"She is not hurt," he said.

"No," I replied, as Deb peeped at him and my mother came up beside us. "No, I thank thee."

He nodded. And then he was away; he had remounted his horse, and they rode on. I looked back at them once as we crossed the field, and my mother saw me.

"A pleasing lad," she said.

"Yes." I felt a blush spread up my face, betraying me.

She laughed then, but kindly, and touched my cheek with a callused hand. "He's not for thee, Susanna."

William

She's a Quaker, I thought.

The girl had not said, "Thank you, sir," as I might have expected, but simply, "I thank thee." And she had not lowered her eyes as young girls are trained to do; as my sister would do in the presence of a man. She had looked up at me with a straight, clear gaze that had no false modesty in it.

I liked that look. And I liked her face, rosy from the cold wind, framed by a dark hood and hat that prevented me from knowing the color of her hair.

I glanced back at her. She was crossing the field: a slight figure, not very tall, gray woolen stockings flicking beneath the hem of her dark skirt as she walked.

I saw now where they were going. There were some farm buildings, and a large barn with people standing around outside it. And I noticed several other groups of people walking toward the barn from different directions across the fields.

"Quakers!" said the merchant. I turned to him and saw a spasm of contempt cross his face. "They breed like maggots in these villages."

The merchant was not an acquaintance of mine. We were simply fellow travelers, having both left an inn outside Brentbridge that morning with our servants to take the road to Hemsbury. I was going home after three years' study with a tutor in Oxford. I was glad of the merchant's company for safety's sake, but that was all. Now, however, I was obliged to listen as he began talking of a Quaker he knew through his business.

"Dismal, canting fellow. Won't drink to your health. Won't attend the company's yearly feast because he says the food should be given to the poor. There's no good fellowship to be had with folk of that sort."

He glanced over his shoulder and added, "Pretty wench, though, back there." He winked at me, and I disliked him all the more.

As we rode on past fields full of new green growth, I thought of the Quakers holding their meeting in the barn. They would sit, I supposed, on benches or bales of hay. I knew they would have no minister. They would sit in silence together until one of them felt moved to speak. And anyone might speak: man or woman, rich or poor. I found it shocking to think of a woman like that girl's mother getting up and playing parson. And yet I was drawn to the silence, the simplicity. It was something I had been thinking about, from time to time, ever since an encounter in Oxford two years ago.

It was a market day in summer, a Saturday, and I was out with some other boys. I was fifteen, and had attached myself to the fringes of a group of boisterous older youths. We had been drinking, and now we mingled with the university students, who were swaggering about town and talking loudly.

I heard a disturbance, and saw that two women had climbed up onto barrels in the marketplace and were preaching to the crowd. They were ordinary-looking women, dressed in sturdy workaday clothes, but not ragged or poor. One was in her twenties, the other older. I couldn't hear properly what they said, nor was I much interested; I heard them speak of God, and the light, and then they must have said something that enraged the university men, who began to shout abuse.

Someone threw a handful of horse dung, which struck the older woman in the face, causing the crowd to howl with delight. I felt a prickle of excitement.

Mud and rotten vegetables began to fly, and then the mob seized both women. They punched and beat them, and we joined in, shouting, laughing, and cheering on the attackers. I was excited, and a little drunk, but not so much that I didn't feel a sense of shame at my behavior. I'd seen fights often enough, but these women were unarmed and unprotected and would not fight, except with words. I knew I should have no part in this, but I was caught by the power of the mob.

At last the constables appeared. By this time the students had dragged the younger woman to a dung heap and thrown her into it. The constables drove the youths back and arrested the women.

They came pushing a path through the crowd, close to where I was standing. The young woman was bedraggled, covered in stinking mess, her face cut and her hair falling down. Her arms were forced behind her back, and the constables pushed her along so that she stumbled repeatedly over the cobbles. The market women looked at her with contempt. "Loudmouthed jade," I heard one of them say. "Her husband should beat her — keep her under control."

I felt the wrong that was being done to the young woman, and yet at the same time I was afraid of her and of whatever inner strength upheld her. Was she mad? Certainly she looked it in her disheveled state, as she turned to glare into the jeering crowd.

And then her eyes fixed on me. For an instant, before the constable pushed her onward, the piercing, bloodshot eyes stared straight into mine. I shrank back. I thought she would curse or spit at me. But she did neither. "Take heed," she said, "of the light within."

Then she was jerked away.

Later I heard that the women were Quakers, that next day they harangued the professors at the university and were arrested again and publicly flogged and sent out of town. I saw nothing of this, but the woman's words stayed with me: "Take heed of the light within."

Why had she spoken? Why to me? Did she see something in me that I had not recognized in myself?

These thoughts returned to me now as the countryside around us grew increasingly familiar and I began to think of home. On either side the fields rose high, nibbled smooth by sheep and broken by outcrops of rock. It was a different landscape from Oxfordshire: harsh and wild, with a big sky. My spirits rose as I recognized the shapes of familiar hills and saw, in the distance, the walls of Hemsbury.

Ned, my father's servant, was riding just behind me. I looked back, and smiled. "Soon be home."

The town was quiet, this being Sunday, and our horses' hooves rang on the cobbles. My father's house is on the corner of High Street and Butcher's Row, in the center of town, with shops on either side. Ned and I dismounted and walked through the gateway that leads to the courtyard; he took my horse from me and led the two of them toward the stables.

I saw the door of the house open. My sister darted out, yellow skirts caught up in one hand, her face bright. Beside her came our little dog, Milly, barking and wagging her tail.

"Anne!" I called.

She scooped up the dog and hugged me with the animal in her arms. Milly squirmed and licked my chin. Anne giggled. "She's missed you."

"And have you?"

She put on a teasing face. "Sometimes."

Now my father was at the door. I took off my hat and bowed to him.

"Will!" He came forward and threw his arms around me. "You are taller. You've outstripped me!"

It was true; and I'd always thought him tall. I noticed, too, that he was grayer, and a little stooped. It made me feel protective, and as I returned his hug I thought: I must fulfill all his hopes; I must not disappoint him.

16

Susanna

$\mathcal{I}$ could not settle in Meeting. Sometimes everyone enters into the silence and is still and centered. Then the meeting is full gathered, and I have felt its power. More often I feel it gathering around me but have to struggle with my own wandering mind.

That day my mind was all astir. I thought about finding work, who we might ask, what they might say. And there was something else. When I closed my eyes, I saw the face of the young man we had met on the road. It was wrong, I knew, to think of such things in Meeting. I tried to clear my mind. I opened my eyes and focused on the reddened, chapped hands of Martha Streetley as they lay clasped on her apron. The apron was made of unbleached linen, and I studied its weave, noting the pleasing unevenness, the changes of color from beige to greenish to brown, the crumpling where she had wiped her hands on it. But that only led me on to thinking of my father, and the loss of his loom, and so back to thoughts of leaving home.

After the meeting we found that most people already knew of our trouble. Gervase Prior, who farms sixty acres at Stanton, said he would try to buy the loom and bed and give them back to us. John Davies had brought a cockerel with him to replace ours. Alice Randall offered a spare bed if needed — "A frame and posts only, but thou could make hangings for it, Bess."

My mother was in tears at their goodness, but I know she would do the same. We all help one another and pray for each other. When John Davies was moved to stand up during Meeting and speak of "our friend Robert Thorn, who lies in prison at Brentbridge," I felt the power of the Lord and the love of Friends upholding us.

"Susanna wants to go to Hemsbury to work," my mother said — and at once there was discussion. I found all eyes turned on me and felt hot and nervous. Isaac and Deb and I were the only children of Eaton Bellamy Meeting; we'd often wished for less adult attention and more young company.

Hemsbury Meeting will be bigger, I thought; there will be more young ones.

And then someone said, "Mary Faulkner might take her on," and I looked up, eager to hear more.

"Mary is a Friend of Truth," Gervase Prior told us, "a good woman, though she has a proud, high spirit. She runs a bookshop and stationer's in Hemsbury, and there is a printer's workshop attached. Printing was her husband's trade and she has taken it over."

It seemed that Mary had had a maidservant who had been unsuitable; she might be looking for another girl. Martha Streetley was going to Hemsbury and would make inquiries.

So it was to happen, as I had wished. I felt excited and a little fearful. I wondered why the previous maid had been unsuitable, and whether I would be any better. And books? I was a country girl, a dairymaid. I had not seen many books. Like most people, my parents owned only a Bible and the Book of Martyrs. These I had learned to read, but I did not read as well as Isaac, who had spent time at school.

"I should like to see the books," said Isaac, as we walked home. "At school the master used to read to us sometimes from a book of fables. There were pictures of animals, and folk fighting and dancing."

"There is much idleness in books," my mother

said. "Susanna must be guided by Mary Faulkner on what to read, if she goes there."

Isaac and I exchanged a smile behind her back. Our mother was a great enemy of idleness, by which she meant not only a waste of time but temptation to sin. Fighting, we knew, was a sin. Our father would never take up arms to fight. And dancing, too, often led to sin, or so we were told; it was not something we had ever learned to do. There had not been so much of it when we were little, in Oliver Cromwell's time. Maypoles, tree- and well-dressing, even Christmas, had been banned by the Puritan Parliament in those years. But in 1660, when I was thirteen, we had a king again, and everything changed. On May Day that year a great maypole was raised in the village, and a bonfire lit, and folk danced till late into the spring night. Isaac and I went down to the green to watch. The sky darkened to deep blue, and the sparks from the bonfire flew up, and the fiddlers played tunes that made my feet want to dance. Suddenly people joined hands in one big circle, men and women and children all together. A woman with beer on her breath seized my hand and Isaac's and drew us in.

"Everyone must dance this one," she said. "Don't be afraid. It's easy."

And we danced, Isaac and I. Most people were

drunk by then, and it didn't matter that the steps were strange to us at first. Soon I began to feel the rhythm of the dance and the joy of being part of the great circle. It broke up in laughter and clapping, and Isaac and I slipped away and ran home, full of guilty pleasure.

"We must go to Brentbridge," my mother said now, "and ask thy father's blessing on this venture of thine, Susanna."

"Yes," I said, but I felt a shiver of unwillingness. I hated prison visits.

We went on fifth-day.

It's a day's walk there and back; too far for Deb, so Isaac was left at home to mind her, and my mother and I went alone.

It was damp weather, with squalls of rain in the wind, and the road was muddy and full of ruts. We kicked up mud as we walked, and the backs of our skirts were soon spattered with it. When we could, we cut across fields. The way took us not far from Eaton Bellamy, and I thought again of the young man in the fine black hat, and wondered whether he'd been bound for Hemsbury, and whether he lived there. I could not tell from his accent, for he spoke like a scholar. He'd be at ease around Mary Faulkner's books, I thought.

"Art thou dreaming, Su?" my mother asked, and I gave a guilty start and said, " 'Tisn't far now, surely?"

"Four miles or so."

She strode easily, carrying a pack over her shoulders. I had another. We had brought food — bread, cheese, and home-baked pies — and a clean linen shirt, a collar, stockings, and a blanket. Also some money, for prisoners must pay the jailer for food and beer and all their needs.

My mother had spent years like this, visiting prisons, or shut within them herself. I looked at her: small and strong, with a square chin and wide-set blue eyes. Her hair was still dark, for she is some ten years younger than my father.

Does she ever feel fear as I do? I wondered. Does her faith always uphold her?

Brentbridge Castle is a ruin, blown up in the Civil War sixteen years ago. Only the tower remains now, leaning at a dangerous angle. The prison is close by, in a place that was once a barracks.

As soon as we drew near I began to be afraid. In the yard stood a stocks and a whipping post. The yard was churned with mud, and the rain beat down heavily. My mother led me to the entrance and spoke through a grille to a man who let us in and barred the door behind us.

The stench of the prison rose up.

I think this smell is not only filth — blood and excrement and decay — but the smell of fear, of generations of people abandoned without hope of release. It never fails to terrify me.

The jailer — a mean-faced fellow in a greasy jacket — looked through our packs and found no concealed weapons. He led us down steps to a lower level. On the way we passed doors with grilles in them, and through one I saw a man sitting, unshaven and pale, with a book open on a table beside him. These were the cells for those who could afford to pay the jailer. They had chairs and beds.

The basement level was cold and slippery underfoot. We heard a clamor of voices. The jailer let us in, and I became aware of a crowd of people before the door slammed behind us and the stench overcame all other sensation.

I tried not to breathe, fearing sickness. As well as prisoners, there were visitors in the room: a woman with a little boy and a screaming baby that she dandled on one arm; an old woman who rounded on the jailer and began to screech at him about her son's condition. Among this noisy throng I saw my father. The tears came up, choking me, and spilled down my face. I ran and threw my arms around him.

"Susanna," he said. His stubbly chin scratched

my face as he kissed me, and I had to fight an urge to pull away because he smelled different: a prison smell, unhealthy. "Bless thee, child. And thee, wife." He reached out to my mother.

I delved in my pack, relieved to draw back from his smell. "We brought thee a blanket, Dad. But where . . . ?"

I looked around the cell. There were perhaps a dozen prisoners, men and women crowded together, and only two benches, enough for three or four people to sleep on; for the rest, there was straw piled against the walls. In one corner was a bucket that served as a chamber pot.

"Most of us sleep on the floor," my father said.

He looked pale, with dark circles under his eyes. His linen was grimy, and I was glad we had brought a clean shirt and could take the other home to wash.

"They have taken thy loom," my mother said.

"I know. John Davies told me." He smiled. "I have been much visited by Friends from round about. Don't fear, Bess. The Lord will provide."

This seemed the time to tell him of my plans. He gave his blessing, said I was old enough to leave home and that there were Friends in Hemsbury to watch over me.

I looked around at the people crammed into the

24

cell: not chained felons but ordinary folk — debtors, probably, or petty thieves.

"How long will they keep thee here?" I asked, and heard a tremor in my voice.

But he didn't know. He was calm and accepting as ever. He is a small man, slight of build, with a quiet voice; yet he has a strength that commands attention, and I knew he would endure for as long as was needful.

He gazed around at his companions.

"We wait on the Lord, and pray," he said. "Already several here are convinced."

At this a man nearby broke in to tell us how my father had brought him to the truth.

We gave my father the food we had brought, knowing that he would share it with his cellmates. And I thought: If they want to be rid of Quakers, as they call us, this is not the way to do it.

"There may be many more joining us here before long," he said, "when they bring in the new act. And it *will* go through, London Friends say, in the summer."

My mother looked agitated. "I can't believe it will happen! What harm do we do? How can they forbid us to meet?"

He shook his head. "This Parliament is against us. There's trouble to come. Be sure of that."

As we walked home, I thought about what my father had said. I knew little of government and Parliament — it was a faraway thing in London. But I had begun to realize that this Parliament — the Cavalier Parliament, folk called it — which had come in last year, was even more opposed to people like us than the Puritan Parliaments had been.

"Whenever there is unrest," my mother said, "they seek to blame us for it."

"Why?"

"Our beliefs. They fear our ideas because we say the light is in every man and every woman, and we see all equal to one another."

So they will persecute us, I thought. And I wondered what it would be like to live an ordinary life, such as most people live: people who never go to prison, who live their whole lives without ever being beaten or whipped or fined, who don't have to find courage to endure, year after year.

My parents had that courage. They lived in the power of the Lord. But did I? I feared that I could not live up to them, that when the test came I would fail.

William

It was good to be home. When my father remarried, a year after my mother's death, Anne and I feared that everything would change and the house would be refurbished; but our stepmother is a woman of our father's age and did not rush to change things. Now, as she came out and kissed me and led me inside, I saw that the house looked much as it always had: well furnished but homely, the hangings a little faded, the cushions scratched by cats. A great fire blazed in the hearth, and I could smell beef roasting.

But my father's business had prospered, and money had been spent. He is a wool merchant and a man of standing in the town. I noticed a painting of him on the wall, done in oils, and he showed me the artist's sketches for a family portrait, which was to include me.

"We must have your likeness put in, now that you are home," he said.

I had been hearing for months of the sittings for these portraits.

Anne showed me another new possession.

"See! Mother has persuaded Father to buy it!"

A virginal stood at the end of the drawing room, in a window bay. I stepped eagerly across to it. Its polished, dark wood gleamed and felt like satin under my hands. I opened the lid and saw that the keys were new and white. I tried them, played a snippet of "Bonny Sweet Robin."

"More!" exclaimed Anne. "Oh, sit down, Will, please, and play for us! We can sing 'The Fair Maid of London' to that tune. Mother has the words."

"My fingers are stiff." I blew on them and rubbed my hands together.

"Have mercy, child," said our stepmother. "Let your brother get warm and take a sip of wine after his journey."

But I was already seated and playing. I love nothing better, and the instrument was a joy. My stepmother produced the song sheet, and I soon had them all singing with me.

We finished, laughing, and Anne said, "Oh, I wish I could play like you! My playing is all clunk, clunk. But, Will, I am having dancing lessons! Mr. Kirkpatrick comes every Wednesday to teach me."

She took a few mincing steps, holding the hand of an imaginary partner, curtsied, and turned.

Our stepmother became firm. "Anne, sit down and do not be so unmannerly."

Meriel came in then with mulled wine and pastries and set them on a table by the fire. I smiled at Anne as she sat, upright and chastened, on her chair. She was only thirteen, although expected to behave like a lady.

Both she and our stepmother were quiet while my father and I talked.

"Mr. Grace sends excellent report of you," he said.

"I enjoyed the scholar's life." I told him about my studies: Latin, Greek, philosophy, mathematics, science. It was what he most wanted to hear about: his investment. For although he'd laid money aside for Anne's dowry, I was the one he had set on a rising course: his eldest child, his only son. He had spared nothing for my education.

He leaned toward me now, enthusiasm in his face. "Will, there's a chance for you in London. You remember Nicholas Barron, the silk merchant? He is moving to London and will be looking for an apprentice later in the year. He thinks well of what he has heard of you and wants to meet you."

"London?" This was what I wanted, to work in London.

"Yes. I'd be sorry to let you go so far, of course — but it's an opportunity. Barron has done well for himself; he has connections in Bruges, Antwerp, and Venice. You'd be able to travel. The bond would cost me eight hundred pounds, but it could set you up in a fine way of business."

I was not thinking of business. I was imagining Venice.

I smiled, and he said, "I see the idea pleases you. And we'd have some months together before you went. What do you say?"

"I'd like to meet Mr. Barron."

He reached over and seized my hand. "You'll like him, Will. He's a good master. And it'd be an excellent connection for us."

My father always seeks connections. He is an alderman of the town, and had launched into his civic duties with the same enthusiasm he applied to everything. He soon began telling me about them.

"The riffraff society produces!" he said. "You wouldn't believe it, Will: the idleness, thievery, drunkenness . . ."

"Oh, I would, Father," I said, and laughed. "Oxford is worse than Hemsbury."

"And do they get the fanatics, too? I was in court the other day, and saw a fellow up before Justice Parkes. The man was a Ranter, or Quaker, or some such, accused of causing an affray in church —"

"In *church*?"

"Yes! They go there on purpose to cause trouble — challenge the priest, interrupt the sermon. Arrogant fellow, this one! Kept his hat on in court. Refused to take it off. Stood there in his hat, answering the judge back, and theeing and thouing him as if they were equals! The usher snatched his hat off him, the fellow took it back — a most unseemly tug-of-war."

"And what happened to him?" I was not really interested in the man. At the mention of Quakers an image had come into my mind of the girl I had met that morning.

"Oh, he was found guilty, fined. But he won't pay, you know. He'll lie in jail, make a martyr of himself. That's what these people do. There are too many of them about. They meet at the Seven Stars in Cross Street, and other places around. But Parliament is to bring out a new law against them in the next session."

That evening, unpacking in my bedroom, I was at last alone with my thoughts. The excitability and chatter of both Father and Sister had run over me all afternoon; my stepmother had fussed; and the servants had been set to airing sheets and heating a warming-pan for the bed. Meriel had brought hot water and scented soap to my room. And Joan, in the kitchen, had remembered that I love gingerbread and had made some specially.

Now I shut the door on them all. I put my shirts and other spare clothes in the chest, looked in vain for somewhere to arrange a few books, and left them on a chair.

The scholar's life had suited me. But now, it seemed, I was to become a silk merchant's apprentice, my career mapped out already. My father probably had a future bride in mind, too: another connection. For three years I had read and studied and translated, and the world had seemed to expand and become full of possibilities. Now the time had come to channel my life into its adult course. I liked the thought of London and the prospect of travel. But the bond, if it was made, would bind me to Nicholas Barron for seven years. Seven years! I'd be twenty-four. It seemed an eternity.

My window overlooked the street. I opened it and breathed in the cold, still air. A house door opposite opened, and a woman came out. A cat meowed around her feet. She placed a dole-cupboard on the street for vagrants, then reached up to light the lamp above her door. The sky was almost dark, and lights were blooming all along the street. I knew that under the overhang of the upper story, Meriel would have lit ours.

There was no view, but I could smell the river, and I imagined it winding through the town and out to the countryside, field and barn dark under the stars; imagined the Quaker girl asleep, her hair loose but its color still hidden.

That Quaker my father had seen sent to jail had stood up in church and interrupted the priest. Why? What did he have to say that was so urgent, so important that he would risk prison for it?

"They meet at the Seven Stars in Cross Street," my father had said.

And I knew I would go there. Just once. Just to find out.

Susanna

$\mathcal{I}$t was a rare treat for me to go to town. Sometimes a peddler came to the village, and we might buy threads or a thimble or cup from his pack. No trinkets. My mother and I never wore such things. I owned two dark wool skirts and a finer one for special days. This skirt was striped in blue and dark red, and I wore it with a blue bodice that dipped in a V toward the stomach.

My mother was uncertain about what I should wear to meet Mary Faulkner — and then accused herself of light-mindedness for being concerned about such things.

"I think the striped skirt," I said.

"But perhaps it is too fine for a servant."

"I shall not wear it to work in. And folk dress finer in Hemsbury."

She agreed. She found me a plain linen collar to cover the open neckline, an apron, and dark stockings. I put on my only pair of shoes: sturdy brown leather, with plain laces. My hair was hidden beneath a loose hood and a hat.

She stood back and looked at me. "Thou'll do."

"Pretty," said Deb, and my mother frowned.

I wished I could see myself. I'd often wished this. We had no mirror — that would be vanity — but there was a pond in the woodland that backed onto our yard, and sometimes I would look in there, or in a pail of water. I'd see a dark, wavering reflection that never came clear. I knew I had no pockmarks, that my teeth were good, that my hair curled naturally. But on the backs of my hands and arms were faint golden freckles. Once I tried washing these with distilled water of feverfew, but was still freckled afterward.

My mother went with me to Hemsbury. I wanted to go alone, but she was set on meeting Mary Faulkner. We walked halfway there, then got a lift on a cart into the center of the town. I gazed around at the crowds of people, the shops with drop-down counters onto the street, the gloves and purses, linen goods, bolts of wool — Welsh russet, Irish fledge. My mother lingered awhile by the cloth merchants' shops, then asked the way to Broad Street, to the stationer's.

We recognized it by the sign hanging above the door: a painting of a hand and a quill pen. Inside, the shop was dark and smelled of ink and leather. I glanced around and saw stacks of paper, quill pens, slates, notebooks. At the back of the shop were some shelves of books and a step stool to reach them. A man sat at a table there, peering nearsightedly and writing in a ledger. Behind him was a half-open door, and from beyond it we could hear raised voices, one of them a woman's — a masterful voice.

The man looked up at us, and my mother asked for Mary Faulkner. While he went to fetch her, I looked around at the books. Not all were new, and while some had soft leather bindings that made me long to touch them, others were unbound or roughly bound in vellum that had curled.

The door opened at the back of the shop, and Mary Faulkner came in. I saw at once that what I wore was unimportant, that she was one who would see past such things. She was a thin woman of fifty or so in a plain cap and apron, the apron none too clean and a smear of ink on her cheekbone. She was wiping inky hands on a rag and looked irritated, but she smiled when she saw us, and said, "Forgive the noise. I am served by fools. You'll be Elizabeth and Susanna Thorn from Long Aston, come seeking work?"

I felt fascinated by the surroundings, eager to see

more and yet overawed by so much evidence of learning. "I don't know books," I said. "Only dairying and spinning and such."

"Thou need not know books," she said. "Except to sweep the floor around them, and maybe dust them and put them away. Couldst do that, Friend Susanna?"

I lowered my eyes. "Yes." I felt foolish.

"The books" — her gaze lingered on the shelves — "were my husband's joy. But the print works was always our living. Come and see."

The door at the back of the shop led into a long, narrow workshop, full, it seemed to me at first, of machinery, men, noise, and the smells of ink and paper. It was an alien, male world, like no place I had been in before; yet Mary moved easily there, stopping to pick up a page still wet from the press and nodding approval to the burly man who operated it. He hauled on a lever and the press came down; another man retrieved the printed page and inserted a blank one. Mary introduced the men. The big man was John Pardoe; the other her apprentice, Nathaniel Lacon. This younger man looked up, red-faced, and I guessed he was the one Mary had been shouting at.

Mary handed me the leaflet. It was a notice of a cattle auction to be held in town.

"Most of the work is of this sort," she said. "I print for Friends, too: notices and commentaries. I could make more profit if I also printed local sermons, but my conscience would not allow that."

"No books?" I asked. I was disappointed. I'd imagined seeing books made.

"No. My books come by carrier from London, or Oxford or Cambridge. For books you need a binding workshop, and artists to put in the illustrations and paint the colors. Ours is everyday work: handbills, announcements of sales, and suchlike."

The press was at one end of the room. It was made of wood and had a huge upright screw at its center and a lever jutting out to one side. When John Pardoe pulled on the lever, the screw brought down a heavy, flat plate onto the frame holding the page to be printed. I watched as Nathaniel Lacon retrieved the finished page, then daubed the type with ink, using two round, leather-covered pads with wooden handles.

He glanced at me as he laid another sheet of paper on the wooden frame. "This frame is the tympan, and over it" — he demonstrated — "we fix the frisket; that holds the paper in place, see? It all folds down over the forme."

"The forme?"

"The tray of type."

I craned my head to look at the type. "It's back to front."

"Has to be. The printing reverses it."

He smiled at me, and I knew that he was glad to break off work for a moment and talk to a girl, and the thought made me feel both pleased and shy.

I looked around the workshop. All along the sides of the room were racks, drawers, cupboards, baskets of rags, bottles of ink. On a line strung between the press and a low beam were hung pages in different kinds of print. Some I found almost as hard to read as the back-to-front type.

"That's Gothic," said Mary. "We don't use it much, but we have the font." She waved a hand at the racks. "All the fonts are here."

She led us to a table where the man we had met in the shop was now picking up pieces of type from an open cabinet and setting them into a frame. The fiddliness of the task irked me, even to watch, but the man worked fast and seemed not to mind it. He was a small person, not old, but stooped and nearsighted, his fingers stained dark, no doubt from years of inking.

"This is Simon Race," said Mary.

I thought: I shall not remember all their names.

Mary explained to me how the type was set up, page by page, all in reverse, with wooden spacing blocks between the pages.

"Canst read?" she asked.

"I can read the Bible."

"Try this." She handed me a little book.

I read aloud, nervous and trembling, for I knew I was slow. "'*The Pious Prentice* . . . wherein is declared, how they that intend to be prentices, may rightfully enter into that calling; faithfully abide in it; dis . . . discreetly accomplish it—'"

She stopped me. "Thou readst well enough. Keep the book. Thou'll do well to learn it; it speaks for young servants, too. Thou cannot write, I suppose?"

"Only my name."

She nodded. "Thou should learn to write. A woman who can write can keep accounts, and list recipes and inventories, and make sure she's not being cheated. And she can write to her husband when he's away."

I felt astonished, and then inspired. Writing seemed to me a powerful skill, one that few women had mastered, though some could read. And Mary thought me capable of it; that encouraged me.

I turned to my mother. "I could write to *thee*, Mam!"

"I'll teach thee," said Mary. "If thy mother approves?"

"I see no harm in it," my mother said. I sensed that she saw little good in it, either. She looked around at the leaflets hung on the line and the many different messages they must contain, and I knew she felt unlettered and in awe of Mary. "Thou'll take her on, then?" she said.

"Yes, I'll take her if she be willing. As for that, Susanna, thou may do as the apprentices do, and come a-liking, to see if we suit each other. Come for a month. I'll pay thee five shillings and thy keep. We live over the shop. Thou'll share a room with me, but have thy own bed. Does that suit?"

"Yes," I said, and smiled.

I spoke quietly, but I was near to bursting with excitement. A working woman. A wage of my own. And I'd live in town and learn to write.

It suited me well.

William

I found the Seven Stars.

Cross Street is a little twisting street that runs downhill from Broad Street toward the river, and the Seven Stars is halfway down, among shabby houses and shops.

It's a respectable alehouse frequented by artisans, not a place I had ever been to. The street was crowded, for it was Tuesday morning and the shop-keepers had let down their counters. A woman selling fish from a barrow had stopped outside the inn and was shouting her wares. A small crowd soon gathered around her, and that gave me the cover I needed to look around.

Inside the shelter of the inn's doorway someone had nailed a printed notice. It said that the People of God (called Quakers) met within on first-days, both in the morning and the afternoon.

As I was reading it, a maidservant came out and threw some slops into the gutter, which was already beginning to stink of fish. She glanced at me, and I moved away as if I had no interest in the notice. I wondered if she was one of the People of God, as they called themselves. Through the open door the alehouse looked like a simple workingman's place: rough benches and stools, a stone-flagged floor wet from the servant's mop. The meetings, I guessed, would be held in a room beyond, or upstairs. I tried to imagine going in there. It would be difficult, but I had nearly a week to get my courage up.

Before long all thought of Quaker meetings was pushed to the back of my mind. On Wednesday evening my father took me with him to meet with some other merchants for dinner at the Bull. One of them was Nicholas Barron.

I liked him at once. He was a man with the confidence that comes from wealth and position; calmer than my father, and less eager to please. He was soberly but richly dressed, his collar edged with fine Brussels lace, his gloves embroidered in gold.

He told me he was shortly to move to London, to an address near the Tower, and that his trade was expanding. He mentioned Venice and Bruges. He said his former apprentice was to leave and start out on his own, and he was now looking for another youth.

At first I was shy as he questioned me about my studies and the work I had done for my father, but gradually I felt more at ease. Our party was in a room of its own, with a good fire, waited on by the landlord in person, and served with plenty of wine. I began to talk more freely and saw that he liked me. By the end of the evening we had agreed informally to the bond. I could hardly do better, I thought.

My father was in excellent spirits when we returned home. He told my stepmother, "I knew Nick Barron would like my boy! It's all but settled, and just the details to be agreed." He turned to me. "You'll do well — and London is the place to succeed. But make sure you work hard; don't idle your time away in taverns and playhouses."

The thought of London sustained me all week. But on Sunday, when we went to church dressed in our best, I remembered the Quakers, and in the afternoon I made the excuse that I would go for a walk — and went to Cross Street.

I saw several groups of people walking together and knew at once they were Quakers: something about their style of dress, which was unadorned and a little old-fashioned, with tall black hats and plain collars; and their grave manner of talking to each other, straight-backed, with no doffing of hats or bowing, and no hint of precedence, although some were clearly of higher social standing than others.

They went into the Seven Stars, one group after another. I had steeled myself to follow them. I hung back a little behind the last group, who were by now approaching the door, thinking that I could always turn back, then realized to my alarm that others were behind me, that I was caught in the flow. In panic I stepped aside, murmured, "Your pardon, sir," and touched my hand to my hat before realizing that the gesture was inappropriate. They acknowledged me with the merest nod and passed inside, and I walked away down the street disappointed with myself.

I turned at the end and came back up, determined to brave it out. I saw the last few — a family, parents, and two boys — going inside. It would be easier now, alone. The door was closing behind them; I only had to catch it —

"Will!"

The shout made me jump as if caught committing a crime. I sprang away from the door and almost bounded into the street, turning around as I did so.

I didn't recognize the two young men at first. Then I realized they were Jacob Powell and Christopher Harley. We'd been thirteen or so and at school last time we met.

"Jake!" I said. "Kit!"

I swept off my hat and bowed, and they did the same.

Jake clapped me on the shoulder. "We've been following you up the hill, arguing whether it was you or not." He looked disparagingly at the Seven Stars. "Were you about to . . . ?"

"No! I paused to — to glance at the notice there, but it's nothing." I knew I would not go in now; they had given me my excuse.

I drew them away, up the hill.

"You look mighty fine, Jake." I remembered hearing that he had been apprenticed to a local wool merchant a year or two back.

He smiled. "My master flourishes and is good to me."

Kit, it turned out, had been less lucky. He had broken his bond with a Bristol master and had come home to look for another place.

"We're out to drown his sorrows," said Jake, flinging an arm around the other lad's shoulders. "Come with us?"

"On Sunday?" All the taverns I knew of were closed today.

Jake gave me a mocking glance. "You're an innocent, Will. Always were."

He took us to a place in Fish Alley, where a door opened into a house that served beer and food in a back room. Illegal, of course, and crowded. It amused me to think that my father probably had the power to close it down, and yet he might be happier to find me here than at the Quaker meeting.

We ate oysters and beef, and we drank too much, each matching the others with offers to pay for all. We talked loosely, boasted, laughed at nothing. Kit told of the master he had left, who had regularly beaten him for the smallest fault and kept him half-starved, by the sounds of it. "A holy mister," he said bitterly, "all preaching and praying and no charity." Jake, by contrast, seemed to have an easy life: the daughter of the house ready to fall into his arms, the maids having already done so; good meals of beef and pork, the finest bread, wine; and free time in the evenings to spend drinking and gaming or betting on dogs.

"And you, Will?" he asked. "Are you in work?"

"Looking for a master," I said. "I've been at school these three years past. In Oxford."

"Oxford," said Jake. "Now there's a place. Are those Oxford whores as good as they say?"

"Better." I could not admit that I didn't know.

Kit, already well gone in drink, said, "A scholar. Been studying whores."

We laughed, loud enough to make others turn around.

A maid came to clear the dishes. Jake put his arm around her waist. "Here's Kate." He pulled her close.

"You've had too much." She wriggled free.

"What have I had? Not enough of you!"

She laughed and cast a glance at me. "You've brought a friend." And as she leaned across to pick up the plates, I caught the scent of her sweat and saw her breasts moving inside her bodice.

We grew more boastful as we drank. I told stories, much exaggerated, of drinking and gaming in Oxford, and I guessed how their stories must be equally false. But my news of a possible bond with Nicholas Barron impressed them. "Don't hesitate," said Jake. "Take it if it's offered."

At last we stepped out into the fresh air of early evening, arms around each other, still laughing. I'd enjoyed their company, and yet, as I bade them good night with promises to meet again, I knew that I had little in common with these two, less than we'd had as boys. And even then I'd been an outsider.

Susanna

I was homesick at first. I'd been used to sharing a mattress in the loft with Deb, and I missed her warm little body beside me. Mary slept in a four-poster bed with curtains. My bed, a smaller one, was open to the room, but Mary had put a cloth-covered screen around it — "In case a naked bed feels strange to thee." I was grateful for her kindness but still stifled tears in my pillow that night.

Mornings in town were all noise and clatter. I'd wake early to the rattle of cart's wheels over cobbles, the shouts of traders, and the sounds of counters being let down and shutters opened.

My chamber pot had to be emptied into the cesspit in the cellar. The first morning, on my way down the narrow stairs, I met Nathaniel Lacon also carrying a chamber pot and was overcome with embarrassment until he made a joke of it.

I'd never before lived among people who were not family. But Nat (as I soon learned to call him) lived there; he had the room next to ours. He was a young man of twenty or so, short, curly-haired, and with a teasing way about him that unsettled me, for I had been brought up soberly.

The other men arrived around six-thirty and did an hour and a half's work before breakfast, and then we'd eat together, the five of us.

My first task in the morning was to fetch water from the conduit while Mary laid the fire.

All the maids from Broad Street gathered at the conduit to gossip while they waited for water. I'd always drawn water from a well in the back yard, but this was a building, open-sided, with a roof, and in the center the water flowed from pipes. The first time I used it, the girl next to me in line began talking to me. Her name was Em, and she was one of a group of maidservants who all worked in shops nearby. They seemed friendly enough, even when I told them I worked for Mary Faulkner and they realized I was a Quaker. They giggled a lot and chattered in what seemed to me an idle way about their mistresses and their dealings with them. One of them told how she'd been beaten and locked in the cellar, accused of laziness. Another boasted of keeping back a coin or two from the change every time she went shopping. "My mistress never notices," she said. The others rolled their eyes in amazement, spoke of coins counted out one by one.

"What's *your* mistress like?" Em asked me. "I heard she's hard on her servants."

"I only came yesterday," I said, "but I know she is a good woman, and she's been kind to me."

Even so, I hurried back, anxious not to keep Mary waiting. She had a sharp tongue, I'd noticed, in her dealings with the men, and I feared to anger her. I saw that she had opened up the shop and was busy inside. The shop had its own front entrance, but I went through the doorway into the long passage that ran down one side of the building, leading past shop and print works and into the back room, where I set down the pails of water.

Nat was there, teasing one of the cats. From the print room I heard men's voices and the thump of the press.

Nat switched his teasing from the cat to me. "Good morning, pretty maid."

I didn't know what to say, so said nothing.

"Kitty, she ignores me," he told the cat. "I shall die of grief."

I smiled then. "Should thou not be at work?"

"I was on my way back to the workshop when I saw Kitty had a mouse."

"Ugh! Is it alive?"

He held the draggled thing up by its tail. "Not now. Art thou frightened of them?"

"Of mice? No!"

"Cockroaches? Spiders?"

I laughed, shook my head.

"Thou'rt fearless, then."

"No. I fear displeasing Mary."

"Thou need not. She's sharp, but just."

"But . . . why did the other maid leave?"

"Sarah? Idleness. She was always gossiping with the apprentice."

"Thou'rt teasing me again!" But I began to busy myself, took down plates from the shelves and set them on the board, ready for breakfast.

"No. She *was* lazy. And dull-witted. Mary doesn't suffer fools gladly." He grinned. "It's most often me in trouble."

"And the others? What are they like?"

"Simon Race is a pleasant man, easy to work with. He's skilled; Mary values him. He's a widower with a young child that his sister on Castle Street cares for. John Pardoe — the big man who operates the press — I like him well. He's a Quaker."

"And Simon, too?"

"No."

"He goes to the steeple-house?"

Nat must have seen my disapproval, for he smiled and said, "Yes. As many good people do."

I felt myself reproved and was silent.

"Mary's a good mistress," said Nat. "She took me from the orphanage when I was a boy, to work as her printer's devil—"

"Devil?" I was shocked again.

He laughed. "Servant boys who work for printers end up covered in ink and look like devils. Mary taught me everything about the trade—and she taught me to read and write; gave me books to read. She took me on as her apprentice and treated me as if I'd been her own. I turned Quaker because of her."

"Thy term will be up soon, surely?"

"This summer."

"And will thou leave?"

"Yes." His face brightened. "London. That's where I'm bound for."

I wanted to ask him more, but someone called, "Nat?" and the print-room door began to open; he sprang toward it guiltily and went in.

We served the men breakfast at eight o'clock: bread, butter, beer, and slices of venison pie from the shop a few doors down.

I would not join the men at the table as Mary did, but took some bread and beer and sat slightly apart, near the fire. One of the cats — a little striped one — jumped up on my lap and began to turn around and around.

Thou'd best not settle, cat, I thought: I've work to do. But I stroked it, and it purred.

The men ate heartily. I served more venison pie and poured more beer. They all acknowledged me, and Simon Race asked me about my family and said he hoped I'd take to town life. He's kind, I thought, and I knew I should not have prejudged him.

I finished eating before the others and went out to sweep the long passage.

Mary had promised me that one evening we would sit down together and she would show me how to write the letters of the alphabet. Meantime, I spent the rest of that week learning what had to be done around house and shop: the pewter and cutlery scoured with sand, the rooms swept and dusted, water drawn, fires tended; milk, beer, meat, and pies bought. I spent much of my time shopping, and that pleased me. There were different markets most days, for corn, leather, vegetables, or butter; one day there was a cattle market and the streets filled with slowly moving herds and the smell of manure. I would move among the crowds with my basket on my arm and the housekeeping money in my pocket, and when I'd bought the things Mary asked for, I'd go home along different streets, discovering a sweetmeats shop, a stay-maker's, a tailor's, and a glove-maker's, all with their counters on the street and maids and apprentices serving.

Mary had told me that the glovers on High Street, the Minton family, were Friends of Truth. On fifth-day, when I paused there, a tall, fair girl of about eighteen was serving. She smiled, and spoke to me, and I told her I worked at the stationer's.

"Then thou must be Mary Faulkner's new girl?"

"Yes. I started this week."

"And a Friend, I heard?"

"Yes."

"That's good. We are too few our age in Meeting."

I felt flattered to be included in her age, for she seemed a woman grown to me.

"I'm Judith Minton," she said. "I have a sister, Abigail, and two brothers, Thomas and Joseph. Thou'll meet them on first-day, and the other young ones."

"Is it a big meeting?"

"Sixty or so."

My eyes must have widened, for she said, "But not all come every time. Thou'll come?"

"Yes. I will."

※　　※　　※

55

Perhaps I went to morning meeting that first-day. If I did, I don't remember. But I shan't forget the meeting in the afternoon.

I went with Mary and Nat. The meeting was held on Cross Street, at the Seven Stars, an alehouse owned by Friends. The room was behind the inn, with an entrance from the yard.

I stayed close to Mary at first, but then Judith came and drew me away to sit with the other older girls. Her sister, Abigail, with fair hair curling from under her cap, was about twelve; Bridie Hughes was Abigail's friend; Martha Jevons was a solemn-looking girl of fourteen; Kezia, her sister, walked crooked with a withered leg.

The room had benches and stools arranged in a rough circle several rows deep, and an upturned tub on which I supposed someone might stand to speak if the spirit moved them. It seemed a proper place to me after the barn at Eaton Bellamy, though I missed the high-ceilinged space and the scent of hay that for me was always linked to worship. Everyone seemed to have a regular place and moved toward it, including an elderly dog that settled at its master's feet. Judith made space for me on a bench where the girls sat in a line, several rows back, under the eye of a fierce-looking older woman who frowned when Abigail and Bridie began whispering together. The boys sat, as I'd guessed they would, at the back, where they could fidget and tussle and scrape benches until the meeting began to gather and they slowly settled.

The door was still ajar. A few more people arrived and sat down. As the last one came in I noted that it was a man, tall and slim, that he wore a black hat with a gray plume in it — my heart was beating fast even before he sat down on the bench nearest the door, and then I saw that I was right: it was the young man I had met on the road near Eaton Bellamy.

I looked away in confusion, feeling color flood into my face, wondering if Judith could hear the thumping of my heart.

The other girls had noticed him, too. From where we sat, a space between people's heads gave us a window in which his profile was framed: straight nose, downcast eyes, dark hair falling to his shoulders. Abigail nudged her sister, and Judith frowned, but I knew we were all watching him.

Slowly the meeting began to draw together in silence. As one or another felt moved to speak, the silence deepened. But I was not part of it and gave nothing to it. All I could think about was the young man who sat so still by the door, his hands clasped in his lap.

As the meeting drew to a close, there was a rustling

and stirring, the dog woke up and scratched, and we began to move. The young man rose quickly and made for the door.

I was already standing. I had jumped up, unthinking, not wanting to lose him. And at that moment he glanced across the room and saw me, and I knew he had recognized me.

William

$\mathcal{I}$ walked fast, away from Cross Street, before the first of the Quakers began coming out. I didn't want to meet and talk to them, or give anyone my name. No one except her. And I would not shame her by approaching her there.

I knew she had recognized me, and that set a little pulse of excitement beating in my blood. She had stood up, and the color had risen in her face, as I knew it must have done in mine.

I walked along by the river, circled round, and came back into town up Spout Lane. At the top of the lane I saw her, walking toward Broad Street with an older woman. They didn't notice me as I followed some way behind.

Halfway up Broad Street they stopped outside a shop I knew well: Faulkner's bookshop and stationer's; and I realized then that the woman was the Widow Faulkner. She opened the side door and they both disappeared inside.

The stationer's was a familiar place to me, one I had often visited. It would be easy for me to find an excuse to call in.

I'll go there tomorrow, I thought. See her. And speak to her.

Susanna

$\mathcal{I}$ was in the shop when he came in.
My morning chores were done, and Mary and Nat
were busy in the print room, dealing with a big order.

"Thou can mind the shop," Mary had said to me.
"It won't be busy, so take the slate and practice thy
letters."

She had already begun teaching me to write. She
had written out all the letters of the alphabet on a
piece of paper and fixed it to a board, and whenever
I had a moment I would copy some onto my slate.
My efforts were shaky; it was difficult to control
the movement and make the smooth, clear shapes
that Mary drew so easily.

"Practice," she said. "One day it will come."

"And then may I have pen and paper?" I longed
to write with a quill.

"Perhaps the backs of spoiled print runs," she said, and smiled.

I was sitting at the table at the back of the shop, making a careful row of capital *T*s along my slate, when I heard someone come in and looked up.

When I saw him, I was so startled that I dropped the chalk and then trod on it as I jumped to my feet.

"Good morning, mistress."

I was still holding the slate. Hastily I put it down and came forward.

"May I help thee?"

"Perhaps." He seemed ill at ease. I saw that his eyes were a clear gray-green, the lashes dark. "Do you have Playford's music collection?" he asked. "The dance music?"

I went to look. Mary keeps the books in sections under their subjects: history, devotional, medical, and the like. I was not sure where dance music would be, or even whether Mary would sell such stock.

"I can ask," I said, "if thou'll wait."

"No — thank you — another time." He looked directly at me. "We've met before."

"Yes." My heart beat fast.

"I did not expect to see you there, at the meeting."

"I had never been there before."

"Nor I. But you — have you moved? Do you live here now?"

"Yes. I am Mary Faulkner's servant."

There was a shelf near us with account books on it, and bottles of ink and quill pens. He picked up a quill and fiddled with it.

"I came in on Monday, and again yesterday," he said. "You were not here. . . ."

I began to tremble with alarm and expectancy. He had been like me, I realized, watching, hoping. This was not a chance meeting. He had come here on purpose.

I blushed again at the memory of how I had stood up and made him see me. The other girls had noticed; they teased me afterward.

"Yesterday was a market day," I said. "I was about town."

He glanced at the table. "What were you writing?"

I saw with dismay that my slate was there. I didn't want him to see it, but I couldn't lie.

"I am learning to write," I said, looking down in embarrassment, for it made me feel like a child. "Practicing my letters."

He smiled. "That's good. Few women can write much, even . . ."

Even the sort of women you mix with, I thought.

He had made me aware of the difference between us: his learning and his obvious wealth. The dark cloth of his coat was plain but of a fine woolen weave.

He wore lace on his shirt and on the edges of his linen collar. He bought books. I remembered what my mother had said: "He's not for thee, Susanna."

But he likes me, I thought in defiance.

He seemed about to say more, but at that moment the shop door opened, startling both of us. A man — a schoolmaster, by the look of him — came in.

My visitor backed away toward the door, doffed his hat to the teacher, and said to me, "I will call back then, for the book, another day."

As he went out, Mary appeared from the print shop. She attended to the new customer, and I retreated to the kitchen, where I began preparing vegetables for dinner. My hands worked readily at chopping leeks and onions, but my mind was running ahead. He would come back; he had said so.

Later that day, Mary said, "Did I see that sprig of Henry Heywood's in the shop? Young Will?"

Will Heywood.

I hugged his name to me like a gift.

"He was looking for Playford's book," I said. "Dance music."

"Oh!" She led me into the shop again, went straight to a shelf, pulled out a book. "Here it is. Thou may show him if he comes in again."

I had an uncomfortable feeling that she knew what

was afoot, that we were not speaking truth to one another, as honest folk should.

"I thought thou might not sell such things," I said.

"Dost thou disapprove?" Her eyes, blue and worldly-wise, fixed me with a challenge.

"No! I would not . . . but I thought . . ."

I knew that Friends were careful what they sold or made. My mother had told me of a lace-maker, skilled in fancy work, who had changed to making simple edgings after she was convinced of the truth, for it was felt that fine lace was only for show and affectation.

"Some Friends disapprove," said Mary. "But I see no harm in it. Such books are for dancing masters and musicians, not for frolics around a maypole. I lived many years before I was convinced: I danced and sang, and enjoyed making music." She smiled. "The spirit must be allowed to expand in us, not become cramped and narrow."

I began turning the pages of the book. The musical notation meant nothing to me, but I could read the titles: "Cuckolds All a Row," "Fain I Would If I Could," "The Friar and the Nun." They spoke of a world of frivolity far from anything I knew.

Does Will Heywood know these dances? I wondered. And there came into my mind an image of myself dancing with him, turning toward him, our hands touching. Fain I would if I could. . . . I asked Mary, "Who is Henry Heywood?"

"He is a wool merchant, one of the wealthiest men in Hemsbury, and an alderman of the town."

And I had set my sights on his son.

"He is not a Friend, then?"

She laughed, shortly. "No! He is not. But his son . . ."

"He came to Meeting."

"Yes. I was surprised to see him there." She smiled, as if thinking of him kindly. "He wore his hat very low and made off fast afterward. Well, we won't pursue him. He'll come to the truth, if he comes at all, in his own time."

William

$\mathcal{I}$ left the shop and walked across town and out through the postern gate into Castle Hill Fields.

A network of paths encircles the castle and leads down toward the river. It's a place where I often came to play as a child. Now I paced around, angry with myself. I'd done nothing right; she'd think me a fool; or, worse, she'd think I looked down on her because she was a servant, that my interest in her was not honest.

And what had I said? I'd asked about dance music; and Quakers didn't dance, or so I'd heard. People joked about them; she must have thought I was mocking her.

And I hadn't even asked her name.

The day was cold and windy, gleams of sun

alternating with flurries of needle-sharp rain. I made for the shelter of the trees and found the ground littered with twigs and branches that the wind had brought down overnight. I picked up a stem of willow; stroked the tight, soft gray catkins.

I had not asked her name, but I knew now the color of her hair. It was brown; not dark, like mine, but golden-brown, the color of a hazelnut shell. She wore a linen cap set back on her head so that a few strands of hair fell in loose curls around her face, and her skirt and bodice were brown.

The girl and the Quaker meeting had both been on my mind for days, hopelessly mixed. It had been a shock to enter the meeting, to step into such a deep hush and see so many people gathered, and my instinct had been to sit down quickly and not to look around. But I could not be unaware of who was there: as many women as men, and mostly craftsmen and tradespeople. My near neighbor, from his smell, was a tanner. An elderly dog lay asleep across his feet.

I was aware of the girls, too, all in a row, darting glances at me; but I didn't notice her — not then. I avoided their eyes and looked down at my hands.

As the silence grew, I stopped thinking about myself and felt the meeting draw together. I became aware of a power I had never experienced in church; I felt that God was here, among us — no, not among us, within us. Maybe this is what she meant, I thought, that woman in Oxford: The light within is the light of God in each person. And I began to see that if I attended to this light, all would become clear to me.

As the silence grew more intense, some of the people started to shake, and the shaking spread through the company. A man stood up, and his voice broke the silence with almost a palpable feeling of relief, as if a dam had burst. He spoke of the Seed, by which I think he meant what I would call the Word. I listened — or half listened, for his words flowed over me so that I grasped their meaning without needing to attend to each one. It was like being bathed in spring water, and I knew that my eyes had been opened and that all my religion until then had been no more than the observance of forms.

Now I wanted to think about that experience, to ponder its meaning; but my excitement about the girl, my success in finding her, speaking to her, made it difficult. I wanted to go again, to experience another meeting, but I wanted also to be sure that I was going truly to wait on God and not because of her.

And here, as the cold rain began to penetrate my coat, I realized the troubles I might be about to bring upon myself. My father despised the Quakers — and feared them, too, I suspected, as upstarts and troublemakers. It would be illegal for him, as an alderman and a member of the council, to worship anywhere but the Church of England, and he would expect the same compliance of me.

The girl would not worry him. He would regard her as irrelevant.

I went back to the shop the next day. This time I had the dog, Milly, with me. Anne had a cold, and our stepmother would not let her out of doors. She had sent Meriel to the apothecary for some willow-bark to bring down the fever. When I said I would go out, Anne asked me to take Milly.

"She's cross from being shut up indoors."

I didn't want to take the dog. Milly is not a dog for a man to be seen with; she is small and fluffy, but with a snappy manner and a way of running after other dogs that I knew would draw attention to me in the street.

But I could not refuse.

"She loves to be with you," said Anne.

And Milly looked up at me eagerly, wagging her tail.

I half hoped the girl would not be there, so that I could try another time without the dog; but she was.

I opened the shop door, and she saw me, and saw Milly, and smiled in delight.

"Is it thine? It's so pretty!"

She dropped to her knees and stroked Milly, who responded by licking her thoroughly.

I realized that Milly was an asset after all.

"She's my sister's pet."

I kneeled too, and stroked the dog. Our hands were near but did not touch.

She looked up, her face close to mine. Her eyes were dark brown, her skin fair with a few tiny freckles on the bridge of her nose.

"Forgive me," she said, and jumped to her feet. A blush had spread up her face. "I have thy book: Playford."

I followed her to a shelf at the front of the shop, and she put the book in my hands.

"It costs a shilling."

I made a show of looking through the book. I was willing and able to buy it, but when I did so, our encounter would be at an end.

"It's for my sister," I said. "She is having dancing lessons and is much taken with the music. And I like to play."

"These look to be merry tunes."

"They are. And the steps are given, as well as the music."

"I have never learned to dance," she said.

"Is it forbidden?"

"No. Each person must be guided by the light within. Nothing is forbidden."

"Nothing?" I knew the Quakers' reputation, and yet still felt shock at her words, for I had been brought up in a society where authority, not the individual conscience, must be obeyed. A memory came into my mind of an anti-Quaker pamphlet I had seen, with a picture of naked people, men and women together, and a couple embracing in public. "But there are things you won't do?" I said. "You would not swear an oath in court?"

"We try to live in the truth. So we don't lie; our word is our bond. We don't need to swear oaths; they are against Christ's teaching."

"And you'd go to prison rather than swear?"

"Yes. Because it is the truth." She paused. "Thou should speak to our elders. Samuel Minton, or Mary." She turned toward the print-room door, as if to look for her employer. "Mary would answer thee."

"Not now. Tell me about you. What's your name?"

"Susanna Thorn."

"Susanna." It felt good to say it. "I am Will Heywood."

"I know." She smiled. "Mary recognized thee."

This caused me a moment's anxiety. But Mistress Faulkner would hardly report to my father that she had seen me at a Quaker meeting. No Quaker, I felt sure, would pass on information of that sort.

"Tell me about the way you speak," I said. "Why you say 'thee' and 'thou.' It sounds old-fashioned."

"It is," she said. "We say 'thee' or 'thou' to one person; 'you' if there are more than one. People always used to speak that way. Only nowadays the fashion is to say 'you' all the time; and men in authority expect it as their due and think 'thee' is insulting. But we stick with the old ways."

"So as to provoke the authorities?"

I thought my challenge would disconcert her; I half expected her to look down, to defer to me in some way. But she faced me squarely. "They may choose to be provoked, but we don't insult anyone. Respect does not come from forms of address."

"And you believe you are the equal of the priest or the magistrate?"

"We are."

She said it in all innocence. I saw now why men like my father were infuriated by the Quakers.

Milly jumped up at Susanna's skirt. Susanna stroked the dog and looked at me with a hint of laughter. "I like her. But she is not the dog for thee. Thou should have a hound. A greyhound."

"And what —" But someone opened the door at

the back of the shop and I quickly took out the money for the book. I spoke quietly. "May I see you here again?"

"I cannot hinder thee."

"But do you wish —"

A young man — an apprentice, I supposed — had come in.

"Yes," she said. And she looked at me with that straight gaze that had so disarmed me when we first met.

She put the money in a box, and I nodded to the other youth and went out, toward Castle Hill Fields.

When we reached the meadow, I took off Milly's lead and let her run. And I ran, too, and jumped a stile. I felt brimful of energy. I flung a stick for the dog, and when she came racing back with it, I stroked and ruffled her fur and said, "Good girl. Good dog, Milly."

Susanna

When would he come again?

I could think about nothing else for the rest of the day; in my imagination I relived our conversation, saw his hands close to mine as we both kneeled to stroke the little dog, heard his voice, his questions, every word he'd said.

I forgot to fetch the loaves from the baker's, and Mary scolded me. The three of us — Mary, Nat, and I — ate leftover pease pudding for our supper instead.

It was the first time I had disappointed Mary, and I was anxious to regain her good opinion. After supper I washed the dishes without being asked, and then fetched my slate and showed her the rows of letters I'd been copying.

"I've practiced them all now."

"Then thou must begin joining up the letters," she said. "Fetch ink, and paper. I'll show thee."

I hurried to obey, lit an extra candle, and laid paper, ink, and goose-quill on the table for her. She sat down, sharpened the quill with a small knife, and began to write.

Over her shoulder I read: "In the beginning was the Word, and the Word was with God, and the Word was God."

The quill scratched on the paper and the candle cast a pool of light on the familiar sentences that we both knew by heart, and which I loved to hear. "In him was life: and the life was the light of men. And the light shineth in darkness; and the darkness comprehended it not."

I watched how Mary joined the letters, never taking pen from paper until she had completed a word. My father had taught me to write my own name; I memorized the order of the letters till I could see them in my head. But I was clumsy and slow, and until now had expected to have little need in my life for writing.

"Try for thyself. Use the slate," Mary said.

I struggled to copy the words, and she watched me, checking I made the joins correctly.

"Rub it out. Try again."

Several times I wrote as much as would fit on my slate. When at last Mary was satisfied that I was making progress, she blew out the candle and told me to pack the writing things away.

"Thou can practice again tomorrow," she said.

I thought of the shop, and Will Heywood.

"May I mind the shop tomorrow? Use the table?"

I feared I was blushing and was glad of the concealing shadows in the candlelit room.

"Yes," she said. "When thy other tasks are done. It would be a help to me."

Next morning I was at the conduit early.

"You're brisk today," said Em, as we walked back along the street together. She was puffing as she hurried to keep up with me.

"I need to get back and do my work. Then I can serve in the shop."

"*I'd* rather be out." She gave me a smile that spoke of secrets. Em was being courted by a shoemaker's apprentice, and they often contrived to meet around town.

"I'm learning to write," I said. "My mistress is teaching me."

"Your *mistress*? Why would she teach you that? Why not something useful?"

It was impossible to explain. I knew she thought me strange, with a mistress who was probably leading me into unwomanly ways. But Will Heywood approved; he had said so.

I waited nearly all day in the shop, and he never came.

I wrote out the beginning of John's gospel over and over on the slate. I made a promise with myself that I would not look up until I reached the bottom line and then, when I did, he would be there, in the doorway. I tried this several times, but each time it failed me.

For a while I left my writing and wandered among the bookshelves. I read a little from an herbal, and looked at the pictures. Many other books were in Latin, which I could not read. But Will Heywood would be able to read them, I knew. I felt the weight of difference between us. How could he be interested in me? Perhaps I had misunderstood the manners of the merchant class. Perhaps he had meant only to buy the dance music, and the rest was politeness — or worse, no more than flirtation with a maidservant.

I was in low spirits all evening.

But next day, before I had even started writing, he was there.

I jumped up, unable to conceal my joy.

"Are you busy?" He looked around the shop, which was empty of customers.

"No. As thou can see . . ."

We both laughed. He'd been helping his father yesterday, he said, with an urgent order; and then later, when he came by, I was not in the shop. My fears had been for nothing; they vanished like dew in the morning.

There was no pretense, this time, that he had come to buy anything. The shop was quiet and we talked for a long time before anyone interrupted us. I'd never talked so much to anyone before. He asked me about my parents' faith, and I found myself telling him that my mother had been brought up a Puritan; that my father had fought for Parliament in the war and afterward turned against all fighting; that I'd been born on a commune near Bristol, where my parents lived for a while before returning to Shropshire.

"A commune?"

"Yes. They held all land and goods in common and were answerable to no master." That was what I had come to understand afterward. All it had meant to me at the time was freedom to run wild and get as dirty as the boys and no one minding. "They were seekers," I explained. "All the time they were looking for a new way of life. A just way."

"And they found the Quakers?"

"Yes."

I told him of a memory of being swept along with my parents — Isaac riding on my father's shoulders — in a great crowd of people going out into the fields to worship because the house and even the street were not big enough to contain us all. His eyes shone at the vision.

"That's how it should be!" he said.

His father, too, had fought in the Civil War.

"But *he* fought for the king. He was much grieved by the war, by its outcome. Most were, in these parts."

"Hast thou always lived hereabouts?"

"The house is the only home I remember. My mother inherited it from an uncle. It has the shop and warehouse below."

"And thy mother?"

I saw I had touched on a place of pain.

"She died when I was twelve. I miss her. My father is full of outward life: schemes and plans. He seeks money and respectability. My mother thought more of the spirit. She was of a faith as unpopular as yours. A Catholic."

I was startled. "A recusant?"

I knew that Catholics who refused to attend Anglican services could suffer severe penalties.

"No!" he said at once. "Oh, no. She was always a dutiful wife and went to church with my father. She would not shame him. But I remember there was a drawer where she kept some things: a cross, a rosary. When she was dying, my father put the rosary in her hands and sent for a priest to come secretly and give her the last rites. He risked that for her at the end."

I thought of the Catholics with their outward signs, the trappings of superstition: candles, beads, priests. Popery was the very opposite of the inward light. And yet . . .

"You are like her, I think?"

He nodded. "She thought much on God. She was not learned, not educated — but she had wisdom."

The shop door opened, and some customers came in. He moved away and browsed among the books until I had finished serving them. After that we talked more, and he didn't leave until Mary came in from the print room and said she would look after the shop now. Then he bade us both good day.

I looked for him at Meeting next day, but he was not there, and I felt bereft. Then on second-day he came into the shop again.

Mary allowed me to serve in the shop most after-noons the following week. I think she must have noticed how often Will came in, but she said nothing, and I made sure I did not neglect my work.

On fourth-day Will found me writing with a quill.

"You have finished with the slate?"

"Yes!" I felt pleased with myself. "I am allowed scrap paper now."

I showed him my work, and we leaned together over the table. I liked this. I was conscious of the nearness of his body, of his breath on my cheek.

"It's not so easy as the chalk," I admitted. "This quill—"

"You must learn to hold it correctly. Place it so, resting against the second finger. . . ."

He took hold of my right hand. It was the first time he'd touched me, and we were both aware of it.

I became afraid of the feelings we'd stirred up. "I have rough hands," I said. "A servant's."

He kept hold of me. "They are good hands. Hard-working and independent."

"And thine show years of study." His were a scholar's, ink-stained and with a callus near the knuckle of his second finger where the pen rubbed.

He was still holding my hand, but let it go quickly at a sound from the print-room door. It was Nat, who bounced in, saw us, and retreated with a wink. We drew apart and smiled.

"Nat will tease me," I said.

He looked at me, and I knew he wanted to touch me again, and I felt a longing to touch him. But a shyness had come between us.

He picked up one of the scraps of paper I had been using for my writing practice.

"What's this?" He read aloud: "'Susanna . . . Susanna Thorn . . .'"

"Oh! Don't look!" I snatched it away. "I was practicing my signature." I felt suddenly bold, and said, "Write *thy* name. I want to see it."

He took the paper back, laid it flat, and wrote "William Heywood," plainly the first time, and then again, signed with a flourish and many twists and curls, so that we both laughed.

I wrote to my mother next day, with help from Mary. It was easy to think of the words, much harder to turn them into written forms. In the end, I said little. I told my mother I was well, sent love to my brother and sister, and to my father in prison.

I realized what a great leap of understanding lay between my reading and writing and Will's. And yet I was determined to bridge it. I read all the Friends' newsletters and commentaries that Mary printed. I read of Mary Fisher's journey to Constantinople to take the Word of God to the sultan, how he received her kindly and listened to her. And I read of the recent executions by hanging of English Friends in Massachusetts, and of the news that Charles Stuart, the king, had sent an order to the American colony that no more Quakers were to be executed by them, that if they were accused, they must be sent home to England for trial. I asked Mary to show me the English colonies on a map. I was amazed at the vastness of America and the great expanse of sea that Friends had traveled across.

One day Will came in and found me reading my little book, *The Pious Prentice*.

"What have you there?"

I handed it to him. "It's advice on how to behave in thy master's house."

He opened it, grinned, and read, mock-solemn: "'From thievish pilfering let thy hands be free.'"

I started to laugh. "Thou'rt disrespectful."

"Disrespectful? Me? Listen to this" — he put on a fierce face — "'. . . the threatenings terrifying them if they walk not according to these precepts.'"

"Give it to me!" I pounced and seized the book, and darted away; he chased me, I squealed, and we wrestled for it, laughing. They must have heard us in the print room.

"You should read poetry," he said, "not this stuff."

"Poetry?"

We stood, not touching now, but still breathless, aware of each other's bodies.

"Poetry." He mimicked my suspicious tone. "Have you never read any? Is it frowned upon?"

"I think my father would feel it might . . . lead to unsuitable thought. It's a thing for scholars and gentlemen, is it not?"

"I'll lend you some," he said, "and you shall see for yourself. John Donne — no, George Herbert. Herbert was a godly man, a parish priest, much revered."

A priest. I felt I was entering dangerous lands. And yet I had been taught that the light was within everyone, that I should seek it and respond to it. Perhaps I should hear what this priest had to say.

Later that day Mary called me to her. I went, expecting a scolding for my noisy behavior with Will. I knew she liked Will, and did not mind him coming to the shop, and indeed would sometimes talk with him herself about religion and answer his questions. But now I sensed trouble.

"Thy month's trial is almost up," she said.

I began to tremble. It was worse than I'd feared. I had angered her; she would dismiss me.

"I'll be pleased to keep thee on, if thou'rt willing."

"Oh, yes!"

I think she saw how relieved I was, for her mouth twitched in a smile. "Good. Then shall we agree a year's service?"

I thanked her and turned to go, but she stopped me.

"When thou'rt minding the shop, I expect thy behavior to be seemly."

I hung my head. "I'm sorry. It was a game."

"Oh, I know these games. But the shop is not the place for them. I see thou'rt much taken with young Will. No need to blush. It's natural enough. But — have a care."

"Will means me no dishonor."

"I know that. It was thy heart I was thinking of. You are both very young, and Will's father is a man of wealth and position."

I lifted my chin. "Will cares nothing for that."

"Then *thou* must have a care," said Mary.

But I could not. Will began seeking me out when I was about town. My heart would leap whenever I saw him, and my feelings must have shown in my face. I read the poems he gave me, and talked to him about their meaning, and found light in them.

Alone, in the shop, I copied out his name and mine. I thought of his face, his eyes, the sound of his voice. At work around the house, and especially in my bed at night, I imagined being kissed by him, imagined his arms around me. I tried to stop these thoughts, remembering Mary's warning, and my mother's, too, but could not. It was like being swept away in a fast river.

William

I thought about her all the time; imagined being alone with her, being free to touch, to kiss. The strength of my feelings took me by surprise; I had known nothing like it before.

But I had to keep her secret. I knew my father would see any connection with a servant girl as beneath me, and if he found out she was a Quaker, he would be furious. And yet I sought her out, not just in the safety of Mary's shop, but around the town.

In the street I was at risk of being seen by our servants, by my father's friends and workpeople, by Anne and my stepmother, who were often about town, shopping and visiting, and would be much quicker to notice what was going on than my father.

And yet somehow the fear of discovery added to my excitement. I soon began to know where I might catch sight of her: at the baker's, the butcher's, around the stalls on market days. And sometimes, dangerously and enticingly, near my home, at the Mintons', the glover's. The Mintons were Quakers, and she had become friendly with the eldest daughter, Judith. There was another girl I saw her with a few times: a sharp-eyed maidservant with a worldly-wise air about her. I kept well away from that one.

We never spoke for long when we met outside. Often no more than a look passed between us. I felt this secretiveness was wrong, that it demeaned her, that I should acknowledge her in public. And yet, if truth be told, I enjoyed the snatched meetings and glances; it made her more alluring.

One day I saw her when I was on my way to a sitting for the family portrait. Some musicians were playing in the street, and a crowd had gathered around them. There was a fiddler, two or three men with flutes and a drum, someone singing, and another taking a hat around. They played a lively tune, and people began to beat time and clap.

Susanna was with her servant friend, on the fringe of the crowd, both of them peering to see between the heads. The singer's voice was bold and strong, the words bawdy. The onlookers roared out the choruses. I saw the other girl laugh, and turn to Susanna; and Susanna shake her head and move away.

Later, in the shop, we talked about it.

"My parents would not approve of such songs," she said.

"Because of the words?"

"Yes, that. But the music, too. Music excites the passions, leads to licentiousness. So they say."

Her color rose, but she held my gaze. It was one of the things that had first drawn me to her, this mixture of modesty and straightforwardness. She was innocent, but not ignorant; and I knew she was thinking, as I was, of the words of the song we had heard, and their meaning.

"But not all music is so base," I said. "There is much fine music in the world. I don't think I could bear to give it up. Are Quakers entirely against it?"

I felt so much drawn to these people that I longed to reconcile the two.

"Many are," she said. "Thou should talk to Mary. She was brought up with music, like thee."

"But does she play it now?"

"She has no instrument that I know of. And little time."

"I think I would always have time for music," I said.

She nodded. "Sometimes when I hear music playing, I long to dance, and I do wonder whether it is such a wrong thing to do. . . ."

*   *   *

For the next two weeks I did not return to the Seven Stars. I wanted to know whether the power of the silent meeting had been a true experience, and I knew the presence of Susanna would be a distraction. So I found another meeting.

One day I rode out alone to Haydon Green, a village to the north of Hemsbury, where meetings were held in the parlor of a large farmhouse. Strangely, it was my father who told me of it, mentioning the place, in a voice of outrage, as a "nest of fanatics" where some Quakers had recently taken a stand against church tithes.

I found no fanatics, only silence and a sense of rightness and people of goodwill. I began to feel that I had not been mistaken, that this was where I belonged.

My father asked me once where I had been, and I said, "Out riding in the countryside," and spoke of the spring air, the lambs in the fields. I was deceiving him with half-truths, but I knew I needed to become clear in my own mind before I challenged him.

The days were lengthening. Sometimes I saw couples — servants and young working people — walking together by the river or about the town; and I longed to go out with Susanna in the easy way that they did, walking hand in hand and sidling off into a copse or a disused barn to kiss and caress. But they were equals; in time, if they loved each other, or the girl was with child, they would marry. My father would never allow me to marry Susanna, so I must rein in my feelings and take care not to compromise her. We could not be seen out alone together.

But I saw her on first-days. I began going to the meetings at the Seven Stars, and talked to the elders and made friends with the young ones, Nat Lacon, Daniel Kite, Tom Minton. From them I heard that the new act outlawing religious gatherings was due to come into force in May. I saw that soon I must give up my new secret life or confront my father, but the thought of such a confrontation made me afraid. He was a man of powerful will, and I had never before disobeyed him in any important matter.

Susanna

"*I* see you've hooked yourself a fine young gentleman," said Em.

The two of us were making our way up Broad Street with our pails of water on yokes over our shoulders. I stopped — and it was more than the weight of water making me breathless. I stared at her. How could she know about Will?

She burst out laughing. "Did you think it was a secret? I've seen him ogling you in the street. And he comes to your shop, doesn't he?"

"He's a scholar," I said. "He buys books and paper. . . ."

"Is that all he buys?" She shot me a sly look. "He's wealthy, that one. Don't sell yourself cheap, Su."

"What do you mean?" My heart beat fast.

"You know," she said.

I did. Em seemed to run a system of barter with her own young man. If he bought her some lace or a bunch of silk ribbons, she'd reward him by allowing his hand to go a bit farther than usual. I knew because she told me all about her courtship, the bargains and quarrels and makings-up. It was something I would never have dreamed of talking about myself, but I was fascinated by the day-to-day ebb and flow of her romance and its matter-of-fact details. They would marry in due course, once he was settled in business and could afford to do so; and, since she was good-natured and practical, no doubt they'd be happy enough. But it was not for me. I wanted love.

"He'll never marry you," said Em, "so you might as well get what you can out of him now. Ask for a love token, something gold. *I* would." She gave me a sharp look. "Or did you imagine you'd be wed?"

I was silent. I would not lie to her.

"Oh, Su! Don't look so downhearted!" She stopped and turned to face me. "I only meant to warn you; you're such an innocent. These grand folk, they'll take anything that's offered, but they don't marry girls like us. Truly, they don't."

Will is different, I thought. But would he marry me? For a girl there is only marriage or dishonor. Or parting — but I couldn't bear to think of that. I tried to disregard Em's words, but she had made me see the world as a mercenary place in which love counted for little.

Later that morning, stepping out of the baker's with a basket of fresh-baked loaves, I came face to face with Will and two gallants who seemed to be his friends. Very fine they were: lace on their shirts, feathers in their hats, and their shoes tied with ribbon. Will gave me a nod, so slight that only I could see it, and they passed on, taking up the whole width of the pavement and talking loudly and laughing.

I felt a pang then, for I saw that here was a whole part of his life that I knew nothing of, in which he would not include me. I should have been grateful to him for not speaking, for it would have shamed me; and yet I resented it, the more so because of what Em had said.

When he came into the shop that afternoon, I was in low spirits. I treated him like a customer and kept a distance from him. He was puzzled and hurt, I could see, but I felt unable to hide my feelings.

"How have I offended you?" he asked.

"Thou hast not."

"Then what . . . ?"

I had turned away from him, and he stepped in front to face me.

I could not explain to him what was on my mind,

so I told him about another thing that had begun to trouble me these last few days.

"In May they will pass the new act."

"The Quaker Act? Yes." He frowned. "My father knows nothing yet of my going to meetings. Or of you. But — it shan't stop me."

"Will! It means breaking the law. No more than five people over sixteen years old may assemble for non-Anglican worship. That's what it will say. Only five. They mean to outlaw us altogether. Thou could be arrested."

"I'm not afraid of that."

"Thou'rt afraid to tell thy father!"

"I'm not!" But he wouldn't meet my eye.

"We will become an illegal people," I said. "It will not be wise for thee to associate with us."

I had not thought much about all this before, but now it became clear to me: the gulf that was opening between us. I felt the inevitability of it, and tears stood in my eyes, ready to fall.

"Susanna." He put his arms around me, kissed my hair and then my face. I swung between delight and terror that someone would come in. The tears ran down my face and he kissed them away and pulled me close.

"Don't cry," he said. "We won't be parted. I promise. Don't cry."

I felt his lips touch mine, feather-soft at first, then firmer, warmer, with an eagerness that made me respond and kiss him back. I wondered, fleetingly, if I should do this. Was it wrong if we were not promised in marriage? But I could not bring myself to stop.

The shop door opened, and we sprang apart. He turned away, as if to seek a book, and I went to serve my customer.

Later, when I was alone, I touched my lips with my fingertips and thought about the kiss.

He had said, "We won't be parted." Surely that must mean he loved me?

But he had not dared tell his father about me, or about meeting with Friends. And I knew his father planned for him to become apprenticed to a silk merchant who would take him away to London. It was his duty to obey his father, and he had all the power.

The next day Mary gave me a gold crown coin — my wages for the month. I turned it in my hand; I'd never earned so much before.

"Thou'll be wanting to go home and see thy family," she said.

"Oh, yes!" I felt a rush of longing. My parents, Deb, Isaac — so much had happened since I had seen them last. And my father was out of prison. A Friend from Eaton Bellamy Meeting had brought that news a few days ago, along with a letter in response to the one I had sent my mother; this, written by my father, spoke of their surprise and pleasure at my new skill.

And yet, much as I loved them all, I didn't want to leave Hemsbury now, even for a day. I wanted Will, to be with him at every possible moment, to have more kisses — and there was a fear at the back of my mind that if I wasn't there, he might begin to think about how uneducated I was, how ignorant and unsuited to him.

But I would not be away for long.

"Go on sixth-day," Mary suggested. "Stay the night and return next day."

When I told Will, he asked, "How will you get there?"

"I'll walk."

"Ten miles? Alone?" He looked shocked.

"We always walk. There are plenty of folk on the road. I'll likely get a lift in a farm cart."

"My sister would never go anywhere unaccompanied," he said, and I saw once again how different our lives were.

I liked being on the road, alone and independent. And now it was springtime, the blackthorn was out, and there were primroses and violets by the wayside. The hedges were green and high, and by midsummer they'd be arching over with the pink blossoms of sweetbrier. It was a joy to be out in the clean air and to hear birds singing and see new lambs in the fields. I realized how much I'd missed it. But not the drudgery, I reminded myself, not the heavy work and the loneliness and the narrow-minded neighbors.

I took my wages, hidden in a pocket under my skirt. My parents were glad to see me, and to have the money. My father was at work again, but he had suffered a loss of trade. They wanted to know all about my new life. I must have spoken Will's name more than I meant to, for they soon guessed, and when they heard he was an alderman's son, they were worried.

"I hope Mary takes good care of thee," my mother said.

I knew what sort of care she meant. "Mary is strict," I assured her. "But, Mam, Will is a seeker; he comes to Meeting. He is not out to . . ." I stumbled for words, embarrassed. "He sees me as an equal."

My mother nodded approval, but she was still concerned. "Keep thy heart free," she counseled. "Thou'rt too young for courtship."

"Thou wast young," I said, "when thou met my father. And married him." I knew she'd been less than twenty.

"I was." She glanced at my father, and a smile passed between them.

A picture came into my mind, then, of my father, a soldier in Cromwell's army, and a seeker after the truth, billeted on that farm in Staffordshire where my mother lived under the harsh rule of her Puritan parents. For the first time I saw them as young, like me, and I imagined the quickening of love between them, my mother seizing her chance of freedom.

"It was a time of war," she said, as if she'd seen my thoughts. "Everything was different then."

On May Eve, Mary and Nat and I watched a great maypole go up in the center of town. That evening dozens of young people went out into the woods to gather greenery, and many didn't come back till dawn. All day on May Day there was dancing and drinking around the maypole, and the streets were full of revelers. I looked out for Will, half hoping, half fearing he'd be there. He was not, but he came that evening to a meeting at the Seven Stars.

In our own community of the truth, we had more sober concerns than bringing in the may. We knew that the new act would soon come into force. For some time Friends from other meetings had been visiting to talk and pray with us. Some came from as far away as Birmingham and Bristol. Meetings were now held several times a week, after work, for we all felt a strong need to be together and to wait on the Lord for guidance. Will came to most of these, but he still had not spoken to his father, and I grew afraid once again that when the trouble began he would be forced to leave us, and perhaps to leave me. I didn't know if he had the strength to defy his family.

The day we heard that the Quaker Act had been passed by Parliament, the room at the Seven Stars was full, and extra benches had to be brought in. In the silence that fell upon the company, I felt the strength of our people. Judith's father, Samuel Minton, spoke first. He said our task was to bear witness to the truth. If we met in secret, the authorities might turn a blind eye. "Many of them are good men, unwilling to persecute us," he said. "It's what they want us to do: to go quietly and meet secretly if we must. But to do this would be a denial of the truth." Several others spoke that evening, all against secrecy. We were resolved to meet in the truth and take the consequences.

In the days that followed, some people had visions and spoke prophecies. John Callicott interrupted a sermon at All Saints Church and was arrested. Daniel Kite stripped naked except for a loincloth and walked through the streets on market day, proclaiming the power of the Lord.

Mary was busy with a pamphlet that John Callicott had written. It spoke against the new Quaker Act and also the Licensing Act, which Mary told me had been brought in to prevent the publication of unauthorized pamphlets.

"Our friend John is authorized by the spirit," Mary said, as she took the text to Simon to have the print set up. She did not seek a license.

The next day — it was fifth-day — Friends were out on the streets, preaching and handing out pamphlets to any who would buy them.

On sixth-day morning I was woken by banging in the street below. A vibration went through the building and I realized the banging came from our own door. Then I heard men's voices shouting, "Open up!" and I pushed the screen aside and saw Mary, with a robe thrown over her night shift, heading toward the stairs.

"Who is it?" I got out of bed, frightened already, remembering the day the bailiffs had come to my home.

"The sheriff's men." She put out a hand to me. "Stay here, child. I don't want thee hurt. Thou, too, Nat," she added, as he appeared, barefoot and pulling on a shirt, at the top of the stairs.

"Thou shan't face them alone!" Nat protested.

"Don't argue, boy. Go out the back way, and run up to the Pardoes'. Fetch John."

"I will." He followed her downstairs.

I dressed hurriedly — shift, stays, skirt, bodice — and ran down capless, my hair loose and feet bare. I could not stay there alone with the sounds of violence and argument coming from below.

The print room was full of armed men. They had stormed along the passage when Mary opened the door, and now they were among the tables and around the press, searching out evidence. I suppose most of them could not read and did not know what they were looking for. They scooped up leaflets in handfuls: bills of sale, auction notices, as well as the so-called seditious pamphlets — everything they could lay hands on — and threw them into sacks to be taken away. Two men overturned the compositor's table. Trays of type fell and scattered their contents, and the men stamped on the trays to smash them.

The leader shouted, "Take the sacks out, and clear these shelves!"

I saw Mary place herself in front of the shelves to protect their contents. One man flung her aside, and she fell, catching her shoulder a blow against the press.

I cried out, and they turned to me.

"Here's a maid come to fight us," said another of them. His face leered close to mine. I could see the stubble on his chin and smell his breath.

"Leave my girl!" said Mary, and I knew I had made things harder for her by coming down.

She got to her feet again and tried to reason with them as they stripped the shelves of printing blocks and fonts.

"There is nothing seditious here," she said. "It is work for the citizens and shopkeepers of the town."

But they ignored her, sweeping the shelves clear, smashing and breaking, and I saw how they enjoyed the damage.

All was over in less than half an hour. By the time Nat returned with John Pardoe, the men were on their way out, leaving us to survey the mess and rescue what we could.

Mary looked white and shaken. I knew she had fallen hard against the press. With her gray hair hanging loose, she appeared an old woman, not the strong mistress we knew.

"Why not go upstairs?" I said to her. "The men will set things aright. Let me make some chamomile tea, and a cold compress for thy shoulder."

I went out to the kitchen, got the fire going, set some water on to heat for the tea, and wrung out a cloth in witch hazel and cold water the way I'd seen my mother do it.

When the tea was infusing, I took it upstairs with the cold pad and a bowl of water.

"Thou'rt a good girl," said Mary.

The bruise was swollen and already darkening. I laid the compress on it and held it there to bring the swelling down. When the cloth warmed from her body, I soaked it again and laid it back in place. Some water trickled onto her shift, and I moved the linen away. As I did so, I saw marks on her back: hard ridges of lumpy flesh.

"Thou hast been whipped," I said.

The beating had been more than a woman could expect from husband or father. This was punishment meted out by law. I trembled to see it.

She turned round to face me. "That was long ago — when I was on the road and speaking as the spirit moved me."

I thought of her stripped half-naked, flogged in some marketplace with a crowd looking on. And, not for the first time, I wondered if *I* would be able to endure such treatment, if my faith was strong enough.

"How dost thou bear it?" I asked. "To be shamed like that in public?"

Her answer came without hesitation. "I wait upon God. In the silence, when my mind is turned to the inward light, I have come to a place where there is no shame and no fear. Thou'll find it, Susanna, when needs must. In that place, everything is possible." She smiled. "Except my stays. Canst help me lace them? My shoulder begins to stiffen."

William

"Have you got yourself a woman, Will?"

I stood still, my heart pounding. My father's innocent question filled me with guilt. Had he seen me? Did he know about my visits to Mary's shop?

He faced me across the warehouse, smiling, open-faced. His apprentice, Richard Allday, looked up and grinned.

"A woman?" I repeated stupidly, playing for time.

"Yes. You know." He sketched a shape in the air. "You take a good many walks, and go out in the evenings. And Richard here thought he'd seen you talking to a girl."

I turned sharply to Richard. But he was not to blame. The streets must be full of eyes. And sometime, I knew, I must tell my father everything. But not yet.

"No," I said. "No woman. I meet Jake Powell and Kit Harley, as you know."

I busied myself with my work. There had been a delivery of Welsh wool that morning by pack train, and we were undoing the parcels and checking their contents. The floor was stacked with bales wrapped in sacking. Bars of sunlight lay across the room, lattice-patterned from the high leaded windows, and in the light floated a dense stream of dust particles.

My father's attention remained on me. "We must have some new clothes made for you," he said. "You grow taller and broader." He draped a dark red and gold wool across his arm and shoulder. "This is excellent cloth."

I looked at the fabric and knew it was not for me. Since I'd been mixing with the Quakers, I had begun to change my style of dress. I had borrowed Anne's embroidery scissors and removed the lace from two of my shirts. But I did it clumsily, leaving loose ends of thread, and Meriel came to me a few days later, full of apologies, thinking the shirts had been damaged in the wash. "I considered them too fine," I explained, embarrassed, and she looked at me, uncomprehending. I had a mind also to change the silver-embroidered buttons on one of my coats for something plainer, but that would mean going to the tailor's, and I knew my family would notice.

Now I looked at the luxurious cloth my father showed me, and suggested, "Perhaps in a darker color." I was unpacking a fine herringbone weave in gray, and held it up.

My father frowned. "That's somber stuff! You want to make a show. Now this, with some ribbons put in bunches, London style, and some braid on the sleeves, perhaps red . . ."

"I — I see no need for show," I said awkwardly.

"But men will judge you by your appearance. Be sure of that. And fine clothes are a mark of a man's wealth and position."

I saw how much it mattered to him, that his son should reflect his status. His energy and enthusiasm would wear me down in the end. But not red and gold; I'd hold out against that — perhaps settle for blue.

"We must all have something new for the midsummer dinner," he said. "Everyone will be there — aldermen, councilors, the mayor." He smiled. "It will be good to have you beside me."

My father did not inherit wealth. He was a farmer's younger son, apprenticed to a draper and wool merchant. In this way he learned the trade, and although he has become wealthy, he has never been too grand to work in the warehouse or shop. But he relished his standing in the town, and I was part of his pride: his clever son, who had studied the classics, who would bring him more honor.

I knew I should tell him about my association with the Quakers before gossip reached him. But how to begin? He was not interested in religion, except as a form of behavior. Anne and I were dutiful children: at morning and night we kneeled to him and received his blessing; at mealtimes we all offered thanks to God. But we never spoke of religion and what it meant to us.

And now I had found a faith that challenged me to overturn my life. I had been shown a new way to live, and, no matter how difficult and dangerous it might be, I knew I must meet that challenge.

I rehearsed in my mind what I would say. "Father, I have begun attending meetings of the Quakers. . . ." The thought of his incomprehension and the pain I would cause him daunted me. But there was no avoiding it.

I will tell him tonight, I thought, after supper.

When I went to the bookshop later that morning, I found it closed. At once I felt uneasy. I hesitated, then knocked at the side door. Nat answered it. His hair and clothes were dusty, and there was ink on his hands.

"Will!" he said. "Come in. Quick." And he shut the door behind me.

"What's happened?"

"We were raided this morning—"

"Is anyone hurt?" My thoughts flew to Susanna.

"No. Don't fear. But they came when we were still a-bed — broke and scattered the fonts and tossed work around. We need all hands to get the print room working again — none to spare for the shop."

"Can I help?"

"Maybe." He began explaining about the unauthorized pamphlets as we walked down the passage into the kitchen and parlor at the back.

I had never been in this part of the building before, and felt as if I was being admitted into the intimate heart of the place.

Susanna was there, kneading bread on a board, pummeling it with small, strong fists. She looked up, startled, as I came in. There was a smudge of flour on her nose that I wanted to brush off, but I only said, "Susanna! I am glad to see you unharmed."

She wiped floury hands on her apron, offered me beer, which I declined, and glanced shyly from me to Nat. I saw that she felt at a disadvantage, caught here unawares. Even when Nat left us and went to find Mary, she did not come toward me, but returned to her work, shaping two loaves from the dough and placing a damp cloth over them. "I've to take those to the baker's when they're risen," she said.

The yeasty smell of the bread mingled with the scent of herbs and onions. A stew was simmering in a cauldron over the fire, and several cats lay snug against the hearth bricks. Behind Susanna a narrow stairway curved upward. They would go up there, I thought, carrying their candles, at night — Mary, Susanna, and Nat — into some arrangement of rooms and beds familiar only to them. I imagined Susanna in the candlelight, her dark eyes shining, her hair freed from its cap and falling over her shoulders.

Mary came into the kitchen. "Hast thou come to help, friend William?"

"If I can."

She nodded toward a broom propped in the corner. "We have most things back on the shelves and tables now, and the men are sorting it all. But the floor needs sweeping."

"Oh!" Susanna looked shocked. "Thou should not ask . . ." She blushed and fell silent under her mistress's gaze.

As for me, I was glad to sweep, if it kept me there and in Mary's favor. I took the broom and went into the print room.

It was good to be among friends and to feel part of the group. I swept a heap of broken wood into the center of the floor, raising a cloud of dust, then collected the rubbish in panfuls and took it outside to the midden. I dusted the press, sorted a stack of paper, pulling out the crumpled pieces, and put it away. Various broken items I took to Nat for identification.

"That's a compositor's stick. For setting up the line. But it's no good now: Throw it out. That's a type tray. We can salvage that."

He explained the different typefaces to me, and I helped him and Simon sort them while John repaired the leg of one of the tables. Dust filled the air, and we all sneezed constantly as we worked.

Later, the women brought in mugs of beer, and we stood drinking and surveying our efforts.

"What will you do now?" I asked Mary. "Will you dare print more?"

"I think we will hold ourselves in readiness for next week," said Mary. "On first-day there may be trouble."

"You fear arrests?"

"We've heard it will be soon."

"I shall come!"

"No!" she said, and I felt hurt. Hadn't I just demonstrated my willingness to be part of this?

Mary put a hand on my arm. "Come out to the kitchen. I must talk with thee. Susanna! Those loaves will be ready for the baker now."

Susanna glanced from Mary to me.

"Get on, girl," said Mary.

When Susanna had gone, Mary turned to me. She was an intimidating woman: not tall, but with a commanding presence, her gaze steady and without any womanly deference. I guessed that she had been born into a family of some consequence. Certainly she was not in awe of me.

"Hast thou spoken to thy father? Thy stepmother?" she demanded.

"I — I mean to. Tonight."

"Until thou can do that, it would be better to stay away. There are difficult times ahead. Thou'rt very young—"

"But I am convinced!"

"Very young," she continued, "and the child of a powerful man who could justly accuse us of leading thee astray."

"You have not! I have come to it through my own conscience and the leadings of God."

"I believe thee. I have talked with thee and know thou'rt a seeker. And I know thou hast prayed and sought God in the silence. But thy father knows nothing of this. And there is the matter of Susanna. I've seen how it is between you, and others will have noticed, too. It might be said that she enticed thee, and such accusations are dangerous. People are always ready to accuse us of witchcraft."

The idea filled me with horror.

"I would never want to endanger Susanna," I said.

"Then wait. Be clear in thy own mind first. Such clearness will come if thou wait on the Lord and attend to the inward light. Now, don't look so downcast. I have a duty to keep thee from committing thyself too soon. When the time seems right to speak to thy father, that will be *thy* time to bear witness."

That evening friends of my father's came for supper; we played music and sang, and afterward, my father being sleepy with wine and everyone happy, I felt it was not the time to speak out. On Saturday he went to Brentbridge on business and was not home till late.

That night I lay awake, wondering if it was fear that prevented me from speaking to my father: either fear of him or a larger fear, of the great commitment I was about to make. I was afraid of pain, of imprisonment, of the loss of that protection my father's wealth and status gave me; and yet the sense of joy and certainty in the path I had been shown was stronger, and I knew it could overcome all fear. But then I began thinking about Susanna: what to do, whether to tell my father about her before someone else did, what he would say if he understood how I felt about her. I lay sleepless for hours.

On Sunday morning we went to church as usual. I sat between Anne and our stepmother, both dressed in rustling silk and smelling of rose water, and all I could think about was Susanna and what might be happening to her at the Seven Stars.

Susanna

We were an hour into the meeting when we heard them coming.

It had been a tense but powerful gathering. Everyone there knew what might happen and was prepared for it. Some had stayed away: Grace Heron, who was with child and near her time; a few (John Pardoe among them) who had young families, or whose children were sick. And Will: I looked for him, even though I knew Mary had advised him not to come; and when I didn't see him there, I could not help feeling deserted. But the meeting was bigger than usual. I saw many children and several old men and women: one, Elizabeth Sawyer, tiny and bent over like a hoop; and Edward Beale, who often rose and spoke at length but today said only, "The power of the Lord is over all," and let the words fall into the silence.

We girls sat together as usual on our bench near the back. Abigail bit her nails. She whispered to Judith, "Why don't we lock the door?"

"We cannot."

"Why?"

"Ssh."

Because, I thought, someone may wish to join us. A soldier, even. All contain a measure of the light. And I tried to hold on to that thought.

When the moment came, it was almost a relief. We heard tramping feet, voices, then a great bang on the door. Judith, who sat next to me, took hold of my hand, and I took hold of Martha's on my other side, and so we linked up all along the bench and gave each other courage.

The door flew open, and they burst in — a dozen or so, armed with swords and cudgels. Their leader was a fair, stocky man with a bully's face who announced himself Robert Danson, sheriff, and told us we were all under arrest.

Edward Beale stood and asked, "By what authority?"

"This is an illegal meeting under the act newly passed by Parliament."

"We are a peaceable people," said Edward. "We have come here to wait upon God in the silence —"

Danson seized Edward and threw him to the floor.

The old man fell hard. I gasped, and heard the intake of breath throughout the meeting. I was shocked that they would treat an old man so; and frightened, too, as I realized what was to come.

"Seize them all!" cried Danson.

The soldiers began to strike left and right, hitting anyone within reach. They struck people with fists and clubs. I saw Samuel Minton fall, and his wife on top of him. Judith's brother Tom was struck across the face. Hannah Davies, with her child in her arms, was flung toward the door.

We girls were at the far side from the entrance and were trapped there by the crush of people. I felt my breath coming fast and gripped the other girls' hands. All around I heard screams and protests. Edward Beale kneeled and began to pray aloud. Elinor Minton called out, "Stay thy hand, Robert Danson, and let us leave peaceably." The soldiers pushed her aside, reached us, separated us. I felt Judith's hand slip from my grasp, then Martha's. They struck out with their cudgels, called us whores and Devil's spawn. A soldier seized me by the shoulders and pushed me toward the door with a knee in the small of my back. I fell hard against a bench and felt the wind go out of me. I heard children screaming; a boy Deb's age was in a tantrum of fear, beating a tattoo with his feet, his arms straining up toward his mother, who was dragged away. Near me I saw Nat trying to shield old Elizabeth Sawyer as she kneeled and prayed.

"Out! Out!" The soldiers seized Nat, then Elizabeth and me, and pushed and beat us toward the door. As we emerged into the yard, I began to shake and cry. I had not often been beaten. My parents were sparing with the rod, and while I was still young they came to deny all outward weapons; so if they were angry with me, I would be punished with their disapproval. Never had I been used as cruelly as this.

I saw Judith crying, too, but others — the old people, mostly — were calmer. They prayed and called on the Lord and asked the soldiers to listen. This seemed to infuriate Danson; he struck at them and ordered his men to round them up. They began herding a group together in the center of the yard. Edward Beale was there, and Elizabeth Sawyer, Samuel and Elinor Minton, William Jevons, John Callicott. And Mary. My mistress's collar had been pulled awry and she had a graze on her cheekbone. I ran and tried to reach her, but the soldiers forced me back.

People had come out of the houses around to stare and protest.

"Leave them in peace!" a woman shouted. "They do no harm! Look at this, neighbors: little children crying, their mothers beaten . . ." She lifted up the little screaming boy, took the mother by the arm and said, "Come away. You shall come to my house."

The soldiers tried to push her back, but she would not be stopped, and then other neighbors joined in to defend her.

Danson shouted, "Take these to the jail!" and began driving the group of about fifteen people he had gathered out of the yard and down the street. I turned toward the meeting room, but soldiers barred the door, and when those of us who remained tried to gather and talk, they set upon us and forced us out into the street.

Parents and children, husbands and wives, found each other, clung together, and began moving away. Abigail sobbed, "Mam! They've taken my mam!" Her face was all slobbered with tears, and Judith could not comfort her.

Daniel Kite began to call us together. He's a strong young man, a blacksmith, all afire with the spirit — bright blue eyes and a head of springing red-brown curls, a man folk will always take notice of. He took charge easily, now that the elders were gone; brought us into a group, where we joined hands and waited a few minutes in silence before beginning to talk about what to do next.

"We should meet again this afternoon," Daniel said, "at our usual time, and visibly."

"We might be wiser to meet somewhere else," one of the women suggested.

"Friend, they *want* us to hide away. We must meet at our usual place and time, and trust in the Lord."

"And put a notice on the door," Nat agreed, "saying that we will keep the meetings faithfully and regularly."

It was agreed, and the word went around that we would gather again in the afternoon.

"Will thou go?" Judith asked me.

"For sure," I said. But I was afraid, and she must have known it.

"Come home with us," she suggested.

"No — not yet. I have my duties at the shop, and they have taken Mary."

Nat and I went back alone to the print room, which was shut for first-day. It came to me then that perhaps I should have to stay overnight with the Mintons — that if Mary was not released today, it would not be thought seemly for me to stay in the house with Nat. And I thought of Will; at the Mintons' I'd be near his home.

"What will happen to Mary? To the others?"

I asked Nat, as I began cutting up a rabbit pie for dinner. "When will they let them go?"

"They have been taken without a warrant," he said. "They know their rights and will demand to be set free, or to know what the charge is. Of course, Mary can be bailed if she pays a fine. . . ."

"But she won't pay?"

"No. None of them will pay." Nat, usually so light-hearted, looked anxious. "And we could all be in prison soon. But Dan's right: we must not give up our meetings."

When we met in the afternoon, the sheriff's men left us no time to reach the silence but broke in and at once began beating people and hauling them out. Daniel Kite stood up and began to speak in that great voice of his, declaring the fear of the Lord. They seized him and dragged him out with kicks and blows. Judith, beside me, gasped in distress as he was led away. Then Luke Evans rose up in Daniel's place and he, too, was arrested, and then Hannah Davies.

They drove us out into the yard and rounded up about twenty people of all ages and sent them under armed guard to the jail. The rest of us were ordered to go home.

I walked back with Judith and her family to their shop, and Nat came, too. As we rounded the corner into High Street, Will came hurrying toward us. He greeted us all, but I knew it was me he was most relieved to see safe. He fell into step beside me.

"I feared you'd be taken."

"They've taken Mary."

"I saw her. They went by in a big group with soldiers around, herded like beasts. But you — did they hurt you?"

"No. Don't fear."

His eyes searched mine, full of anxiety, and I felt a rush of tears spring up. I said, "I'll lie at the Mintons' tonight, now that Mary's gone."

"Come with us, Will," said Judith. "We'll eat, and talk."

The Mintons' shop, under the sign of the gloved hand, is only a few doors from Will's home. Here, in the center of town, houses and shops are packed close, grand and small together. Next door to the glove-maker's is a tailor's, and on the other side a shoemaker's. The tailor's wife came out when we appeared and asked if we had come to any harm.

"None, I thank thee," said Judith. "But our parents are taken to prison without a warrant."

The woman saw Abigail's tear-stained face and said, "This is a bad business. Your parents are godly folks and good neighbors. They should not be treated so." She reached out to Abigail. "Never fear, pet, we'll get them out. My husband will stand bail for them."

"Thou'rt good to us," said Judith. "But my parents will not agree to it."

"But the children . . ." The woman looked pityingly at Abigail and Joseph. "There is a time to give over stubbornness. We'll go with you tomorrow and see what can be done."

After we had gone in and were upstairs in the rooms above the shop, there came a knock at the door; it was the woman's servant with a dish of meat for us to share and some pottage for the children.

Judith put the food on the table and we gathered around. All the time I was aware of Will, conscious that we had never been together in a group like this before, and that all except perhaps young Joseph must know of our feelings for each other.

There were only two chairs, and Judith offered these to Nat and Will. The rest of us sat on benches. We ate and talked, our discussion full of what might be to come. From time to time I glanced at Will, wondering what he thought of this craftsman's home with its simple furniture and pewter tableware. Even now, dressed in his plainest clothes, he did not look like one of us.

"There are thirty people or more in prison now,"

said Judith. "They cannot keep them long. The over-crowding will be too much."

"They care nothing for that," Nat said. "They'll push us in till there be no more room to stand. It's happening in London, they say. And Bristol. All around."

I thought then of my parents in Long Aston. Would the country meetings be raided, too?

After we had finished eating, Judith cleared the dishes and sent Abigail and Joseph to bed. The men brought the benches closer to the fire, and Will moved swiftly to sit beside me. My heartbeat quickened, and I knew I was blushing. But no one had noticed. Nat was asking Tom about his plans for an apprenticeship. Tom was fourteen, fair and tall like Judith, and more than ready to leave home. His sights were set on Bristol. He spoke eagerly of going there, of how big the Bristol meetings had grown, of the Quaker merchants who were beginning to flourish because they dealt fairly and their word was their bond. "And the docks!" he said. "I'd see the ships that sail to Africa and the New World!"

"Dan Kite has thoughts of sailing to America, to spread the truth there," said Nat.

"He told me," said Judith, and I saw at that moment that she loved Daniel and feared for him and did not want him to go. "But there's more danger in Massachusetts than here, surely?"

I knew she was thinking of the news I'd read about, of Friends hanged in Boston because they defied the law against Quakers entering the colony.

"If so, there is the Lord's work to be done there," said Tom, and Judith said, "Oh, Tom," and sat biting her thumbnail.

"There are other places," Nat said. "They say America is vast beyond imagining — land to be had for the taking."

"The Garden of Eden?" I said, and yawned. I was growing sleepy. The light had gone and Judith had not yet lit candles. We had only the embers of the fire to see by. I was lost in the pleasure of being so close to Will; not touching, but near enough to feel each slight movement as he leaned forward or shifted his weight on the bench. He was quiet, no doubt feeling somewhat of an outsider, but he listened intently. I snatched sidelong glances at him: at his face, the line of cheekbone and jaw lit by the fire's glow, at his hands resting on his thighs. I longed to reach out and take his hand in mine, but a girl could not be so bold.

"Eden had a serpent," said Judith. She shivered. "I should not like to go so far . . . so many months at sea. . . . Would thou go, Nat?"

He laughed. "I'd need earn my passage before even thinking of it. I'm bound for London, as a journeyman printer."

"And thee, Will?" asked Tom.

I looked up sharply at Will's face. His answer was important to me.

"To London," he said, "if the bond is agreed. "But" — he sighed and struck with clenched fists on his knees — "thou knowst how I am torn."

I had never heard him use our way of speech before; and it seemed he had done it without thinking. He is being drawn in, I thought, and I was both glad and fearful for him. I didn't want him to go to London, and yet, if he stayed, he might suffer in prison, and how could I wish that? God will uphold us, I thought, no matter what comes.

The fire was now so low that the walls were almost invisible, and when we stood up, the darkness enfolded us and Nat and Will had to cast about to find their coats and hats. Judith looked out and checked that the Mintons' servant, Hester, had lit the outside light. The shop sign, swinging below the window, creaked in a rising wind.

"I'll walk back with thee, Will," said Nat.

They said goodbye, and Will briefly touched my hand. "I'll come tomorrow."

I shared Judith's bed that night. Both of us were wakeful, aware of her parents' empty chamber and of how uncomfortably they must be lodged, and of Abigail nearby, who made small whimpering sounds in her sleep. We whispered, so as not to wake her.

"I think thou lovst Dan Kite," I said.

"Oh! Is it so clear to see? But what of thee and Will Heywood?"

We laughed and shushed each other.

"But has Dan spoken?" I asked. "Will you be wed?"

"Oh, Su, I don't know! I think he likes me. Indeed, I know he does. But he's a man full of action and schemes and ideas. I don't know if I could live such a bold, outward life. My mother thinks him wild. And she says I'm too young."

"*My* mother was young, like thee, when she married," I said.

I lay thinking of Will, and whether we would ever be married. Would he want me? And if he did, would his family allow it?

"Everything is different," my mother had said, "in a time of war."

It feels like a time of war now, I thought.

William

"*Father* . . ." I took a breath. "Father, I must speak to you about the prisoners."

It was Monday, and we had finished our midday dinner. The women had left us, and we were drinking: small beer, not wine, for my father likes to stay alert for business in the afternoon.

He was alert now — and puzzled.

"Prisoners?"

"The Quaker prisoners. Those who were arrested yesterday."

He stared at me, and I felt myself beginning to tremble with a mixture of anticipation and fear. My father, wearing his hat, as he always did indoors as head of the family, was an intimidating figure.

"They are kept without warrant," I said. "Therefore they don't know why they are detained or when —"

"Don't *know*!" he exploded, and I flinched. "They know exactly why they are detained. They are a most wily people and know everything about the law and how to use it to their advantage. As for the warrant, with so many arrested at once it is bound to take time. . . . But what's your interest in this? Who have you been talking to?"

"I . . . have some friends among them."

"Friends? Among the Quakers? Ah . . ." He leaned back in his chair and regarded me with cynical amusement. "I see it all now. It's this girl, isn't it? The one Richard saw you with. You've got yourself a Quaker girl and now you want her released from jail. Is that it?"

"I have several friends, both male and female."

Abruptly he sat upright; the smile was gone. "Then break with them, Will. I order it. Those people are no right companions for you. They threaten Church and state; they pay no tithes; they refuse to take the oath of allegiance. They are a danger to the constitution and to the very fabric of society. I forbid you to associate with them."

I had never defied him before. It took all my courage to reply. "I find them to be good Christians, sir, who seek the will of God in silence."

"Do you argue with me, boy?" His face flushed red, and I was reminded of times when I was a child and he had beaten me for some fault. He might do so still, if I disobeyed him.

"I have been drawn to them for some years," I said. "In Oxford I heard two women speak —"

"*Women!*" He almost spat the word. "So we are to have women preach to us now?"

"They say — the Quakers say — that we need no hired priests to intervene between ourselves and God, that the light is in everyone."

He made a sound of contempt. "So every fishwife, every pox-ridden whore, is to look into her heart and receive the truth and broadcast it? It's a recipe for chaos, Will. They must be rooted out, and this new law will do it."

"Father, I believe —"

He sprang up then, slamming back his chair. "I care not what you believe! I am an alderman of this town, and you are my son. You will not visit those people again."

I became aware that my stepmother and Anne had stopped talking in the parlor next door, and that Meriel was hovering in the doorway, uncertain whether to come in and clear the table.

"Come in, Meriel," my father said. "I must go back to the shop. And you'll come with me, Will; I'll find you work to do."

I went down the stairs ahead of him, glanced back,

and saw him talking to my stepmother, reassuring her.

He kept me all afternoon in the shop and warehouse. I was not much needed there, but was able to see how Richard kept accounts and dealt with customers. It was useful to me and I would not have resented it, except that I knew my father wanted me under his eye.

That evening, at supper, he was as good-humored as usual. I realized that he considered the matter closed; he had told me what to do and expected me to obey.

I could not, but neither could I find the courage at that moment to confront him again; so I went out, thinking to find Susanna, and he watched me put on my hat and said nothing.

I went first to the Mintons', but Judith told me Susanna was still at Faulkner's, so I made my way there.

It was a warm evening, and the air would have been mild and sweet had it not been for the rank smell from the channel in the middle of the road, which is always worse in such weather. In order to calm myself and clear my thoughts, I took the long way to Broad Street and walked along the town walls. A rosy sunset lit the fields and woods below, but the trees were knots of shadow. I saw a man — a vagrant, probably — settling with his pack in the lee of a hedge, and envied him his freedom.

No one answered my knock at the printer's, so I found a way around the backs of the houses, and came upon Nat and Susanna in the yard. He was washing something in a bucket, while she leaned against the door frame and chatted with him.

They looked so easy together that I felt a stab of jealousy. He lives here, I thought, sleeps in the next room, works with her, prays with her.

Then Susanna looked up and saw me. Her face brightened, she smiled, and I knew I had no cause for fear.

I opened the gate and went in. Nat, I found, was cleaning the ink daubers in a bucket of urine.

He grinned as I stepped back from the smell. "Got to be done. Every night, after a day's use."

He had taken off the leather covers and put them to soak in the urine — "That softens them" — and was clearing the horsehair stuffing of lumps.

He nodded toward the house. "John's still here. We've been working late on a pamphlet for Friends."

"How do they fare, those in prison?" I asked.

I did not want to talk about the prisoners; I wanted to speak to Susanna alone, to tell her what my father had said and how I felt about it. But she and Nat were both angry on behalf of their friends, and Susanna responded with a flash of fire. "There is *still* no warrant, and they don't know when they will come to court! They are crowded together with no room to lie down, and there is only one chamber pot, which all must use, male or female. Judith's mother is so overcome with the foulness she cannot bring herself to eat or drink."

"Can they not be bailed?"

"They will not pay. And will not have others pay for them."

"I spoke to my father," I said. "Asked him why they are kept without authority."

"Thou told him?"

Both turned startled eyes on me. Susanna looked fearful and yet glad. Before I could say more, John Pardoe came out, greeted me, and said he was going home.

"I was to have walked back to the Mintons' with Susanna," he said to me, "but . . ."

"I'll walk with her," I said.

We left soon after, leaving Nat to lock up. The alley was deserted, and when we reached a shadowy corner I put my arms around Susanna and kissed her. It was so long since we'd had a moment alone together that I felt as if I'd been starved. I pulled her closer, feeling the slender curves of her body outlined by her stays.

"Will . . ." She spoke between kisses, her voice low and anxious. "What did thy father say? Does he know about me?"

"He has guessed there is a girl — but don't fear, he doesn't know thee. He has forbidden me to see any of you again."

"And yet thou'rt here."

"Yes."

"Does he know?"

"Not yet. But he will. He must."

We walked the slow way back, along the town walls, where we saw the countryside now almost in darkness, the hills blended with the sky. I held Susanna's hand and wished with all my heart that we could walk like this with my father's blessing. A watchman passed us with his lantern, and as he turned up an alleyway into the town, we heard his call: "Nine o'clock and all's well."

A lamp was shining outside the Mintons' door. We knocked; their servant, Hester, opened it, and Susanna went quickly inside.

I walked the short distance to my own home. The servants were about, but to my relief my father had already gone to bed. I went up to my room and flung myself flat on my back on the bed and gave way to thoughts of Susanna and the feelings she aroused in me. She'd be with the Mintons now, sharing a bed with Judith. Suppose I'd brought Susanna here, to my own bed? I imagined smuggling her in, holding and kissing her as we reached the secrecy of my room; imagined how she'd feel without stays, with her hair loose and falling across my neck and arms.

We must be together, I thought. We must marry; it's the only way. But how? My father would never agree to it. Perhaps the Quakers would marry us. But where would we live? Where could we go? I found no answers.

The next day I had other concerns. After a sleepless night, I had resolved to speak as the Quakers did when I met my family in the morning, using "thee" and "thou." I wanted to prove, to myself as much as to them, that I was convinced of the truth. I was tense and ready for the confrontation this would produce. But then we all met, and in the humdrum exchanges of family talk, I forgot. It was difficult to remember a different way of speaking. I felt foolish, but it was too late to make the change.

In the shop and warehouse that morning, my father and I were both busy, not talking together. But later he sent me out on an errand, and when I returned I saw horses — a pack train — in the yard.

When I went in he was talking to a Welsh merchant he often had dealings with.

"Ah, Will!" he said, and turned to the other man. "Mr. Rhys: you remember my son, William?"

The merchant swept off his hat and bowed to me.

My own hand moved instinctively toward my hat — then I let it fall back. I acknowledged the man's bow with a nod and said, "I'm pleased to meet thee, John Rhys."

He looked surprised, glanced at my father, then back at me, and smiled uncertainly.

My father had turned dark with rage.

"Go home, Will," he said in a low voice. "We'll speak later."

He led the merchant away, remarking, "My son has taken up with some loose people in the town, but . . ." The rest of his words were lost as the two of them moved farther into the warehouse.

I stood trembling. I had dealt with this badly, I knew. I should have confronted my father alone, at home, not here. I had embarrassed him and insulted his visitor. And yet — how else? I was convinced that the Quakers were right, that hat-honor and sweeping bows were nothing but sham and show, that honest men should look each other in the eye and no man should bow to another, since all are equal.

138

But it had been hard to do, and all my instincts were against it, for I had been schooled in polite behavior from my youth.

I did not go home, but out, through the Eastgate and down to the river, where I liked to go to walk and think. But I would not disobey my father more than necessary. I was home when he returned.

Anne had persuaded me to pick out a tune from Playford on the virginal for her and was practicing the dance steps as I played. When my father came and called me out of the room, she stood still, and her frightened glance flicked between the two of us.

I followed my father down to his accounting room, where he keeps the bills and ledgers. He also keeps a rod, and it was here that I used to be summoned for a beating as a child. I tried to remember some of my misdemeanors — small things, easily remedied by a beating: telling a lie, misbehaving in church, not learning my lessons properly, breaking a window with a ball . . . nothing like this. There was no remedy for this.

I heard the pent-up anger in his voice as he said, "You are my son. I hoped — I expected — that you would be a credit to me, that I might be proud of you."

"Father, I meant no disrespect —"

For answer he flung me against the table and ordered me to lean over it.

"I'll teach you respect," he said.

He seized the rod and struck out at me. The blows fell on my back, buttocks, arms, and shoulders, and he grunted with the exertion. I was taller than he was now and could have resisted, but I did not. I clenched my teeth against the pain and made no sound. It was not the pain I minded; it was the humiliation, being treated like a child again, the breaking of the new adult relationship that had been growing between us. By law he was within his rights to beat any of us — child, wife, or servant — but at that moment I hated him for it.

At last his rage was spent. The blows stopped; I heard him breathing heavily. I turned stiffly to face him, and we glowered at each other.

"You will not dare insult my customers again," he said.

I struggled to keep my lips from trembling, to maintain dignity. "I insulted no one. But I *will* dare! I will dare anything for the truth."

He stared at me, and I saw bewilderment in his face as well as anger. He exclaimed in a voice of desperation, "Will, you must sever yourself from these people!"

"I can't. My conscience —"

"Damn your conscience!" He flung the rod into the corner of the room. "You are too much your mother's child, too concerned about your soul; you do too much *thinking*, Will. But your mother knew what came first. She put duty before conscience."

"I can't do that. I must be true. Be a witness."

"Even if your *conscience*" — he spoke the word with a sneer — "ruins your father's business and your own prospects? And your sister's?"

"I shall go to the Quaker meeting next first-day," I said.

At that he looked triumphant. "You will not," he said. "On Thursday I leave for Welshpool, for several days' business, and you will come with me."

Susanna

Our people remained in jail. On fourth-day they were all brought before a magistrate, but he only heard the charges against them and committed them to prison again to await the next sessions.

We visited them every day. Nat would go each morning to ask Mary's wishes about her work and what was to be done. She put him in charge of the print room, and it was he who took orders and made sure the work was delivered on time. It surprised me to see Nat take charge. I'd thought him light-minded and playful — and so he was sometimes — but now he seemed to grow in response to Mary's trust in him.

I went about my tasks in the shop and kitchen, and tried to do all that Mary would have wished. Will did not come the next day, or the one after. I looked for him when I was out at market but did not see him. His home on High Street gave away no secrets. It was a house that turned its back on the town: the windows small and high, and all the life of the place facing inward, onto the courtyard that lay beyond the arched entrance. That powerful man, his father, had forbidden Will to see me again. I feared that he had prevailed, that Will was locked up, or sent away. The other possibility, that he had been persuaded into obedience, I tried not to think about.

When the shop was not busy, I read more from the book of George Herbert's poems that Will had lent me. Some were difficult; others I loved at once and copied out as my handwriting improved. I longed for Will to walk in, to take me in his arms, to read with me, and talk. Surely he loved me and would defy his father for me? I put George Herbert aside, and wrote "Susanna Heywood" on my scrap paper — and then quickly scratched it out for fear someone should see. And I began to think, then, about what might come of our love. I was causing him to quarrel with his family, perhaps to renounce them. If it were not for me, he might never have gone to another meeting, never been led into such danger as we now faced. His family would say I had lured him away from the Anglican Church, and perhaps they were right. I thought of my own loving parents and how I would feel if anything came to cause a rift between us.

And yet I could not give him up. I knew I was not unworthy of him; we were equal before God. And I was determined to learn to write and print and carry the truth to any who would hear it, and be an equal partner to him, if he would have me, if God willed it.

I slept at the Mintons' that week, but came home in the mornings to prepare breakfast for the men and afterward serve in the shop. In the afternoons I met up with Judith and the younger children, and we all went together to the prison.

The Castlegate prison, where our people were held, is in the castle vaults. We could hear the noise as we went down the steps. Despite the smell and overcrowding, our friends talked and received visitors and dictated letters and petitions. All were locked into one room, without means to wash. There was a stinking bucket they had to use as a privy, and the straw on which they lay at night was rank with filth.

Mary's eyes were red from lack of sleep. She was plagued by lice and fleas, and her linen was soon smeared with dirt. On fourth-day I brought her a clean cap and apron, and all the visitors brought food. Most of it was shared in common and passed around: jugs of fresh milk, bread, cheese, and meat.

Judith's neighbor, the tailor, was there; he was

trying for the second time that week to bail out her parents, Samuel and Elinor, but they would not consent to it.

Abigail begged her mother, "Please let him pay. Come out, Mam. Jude, tell Mam to let George Woodall pay."

But Judith shook her off, impatient. She was turning about, looking for someone — and I realized Daniel Kite was not there.

"Where is Dan?" she asked.

"He's in the Pit," said her mother.

I felt shocked. We had all heard about the Pit, where unruly prisoners are kept. It's entered through a hole in the floor; the prisoner must climb down a ladder, which is then drawn up. There is no light or air, the walls run with water, and there are rats.

Judith was desperate. She went to speak to the jailer, and I heard their voices raised. On the way home she told me, "No one can see him. He's chained and manacled like a felon! Oh, Su—" Her voice broke. "We must pray for strength."

That evening, at last, Will came to me.

When Hester called me, I was upstairs, in the Mintons' parlor, and I rushed to the top of the stairs and saw him waiting below in the empty shop.

"Will!"

I ran down the stairs and he came toward me and we caught each other on the lower steps and clung together. There was only one small candle in a niche of the stairwell, so I could not see his face clearly. I felt him flinch when I hugged him, and drew back. "What is it?"

"My father beat me. It's nothing. Don't let go." And he gathered me into his arms. I felt his kisses on my mouth and his body hard against mine; and I was excited and yet frightened because I sensed that he was in the grip of feelings more powerful and urgent than my own, and that I was the cause of them. I struggled, and he released me and held me more gently.

"I could not come before. My father keeps me at work, under his eye." And he told me how he had challenged his father and been punished for it.

"I have to go away tomorrow," he said. "My father is going to Welshpool to buy wool, and I must go with him."

"How long?" I breathed in the smell of him: a sharp male scent mixed with the soap and lavender of his linen, which was always new-laundered and pleasing to me. I couldn't bear it, I thought, if he went away. And Welshpool was far off.

"He won't say. A few days, I expect. He means to keep me from Meeting on first-day. And he thinks I'm at home now. I must go back."

But he didn't go, not at once. We stayed there on the stairs and kissed and whispered and caressed until sounds of creaking floorboards from above reminded me that it was late and the others would be going to bed.

We drew apart, and he kissed me one last time, his face and lips hot against mine.

"I *will* come back," he promised. "My father shan't keep us apart."

When he was gone, I felt warm, excited, and unhappy all at once. I straightened my collar, tucked strands of hair under the edge of my cap, and ran upstairs. Judith was already in bed, and I undressed quickly to my shift and squeezed in beside her. Her hair tickled my face as she rolled over and put her arms around me. Her face was wet.

"Thou'rt crying," I said.

Judith sniffed. "I fear for Dan," she said, "and my parents, and how I'll manage the younger ones — Abby especially. Oh, Su! Don't *thou* cry, too."

I told her Will's news, burrowing against her. "He's in such trouble with his father, and I fear we'll never be together."

"Better for Will if he's not here on first-day," said Judith. "The authorities are sure to come back. They are breaking up meetings all around."

I thought of my parents at Eaton Bellamy Meeting. We expected any day to hear of their arrest.

"Dost thou think they'll arrest us all tomorrow?"

"Not thee. Thou'rt too young."

"'Persons over sixteen years'," I said, remembering Mary reading out the act to us. "I might be taken for sixteen."

"No. Thou'rt young in thy looks, and small. And Tom's scarce fourteen, and the others just children."

"Perhaps they won't come," I said. "Perhaps they have seen that we are not afraid to meet."

"They'll come," said Judith.

They came soon after we had gathered, when John Pardoe was on his feet and speaking. They burst in as before with cudgels and swords, and when John demanded to see a warrant, Robert Danson drew his sword with a cold scrape of metal and pointed it at John's belly. "This is my warrant," he said.

It was over quickly. They took all the adults: John and Nat and several old women. They tore Abigail's hands from her sister's and arrested Judith. I watched in despair as my friends Nat and Judith were taken from me and driven out into the street and marched away. Tom and Joe ran at the soldiers and tried to stop them, but the men jeered and prodded them back with the points of their swords. One of them seized Joe's hat and filled it full of horse dung and slapped it back on his head. The lad pulled it off, but the mess was all in his hair and they laughed at his distress.

Soldiers stood guarding the door of the meeting room. We tried to gather in the courtyard, but they drove us out with threats and curses. There was nothing we could do but go.

Back at the Mintons', Hester cried out, "Oh, what have they done to thee, child?" and hauled Joe away to be washed. As she doused him with cold water, ignoring his yells, she said, "You won't go back there after noon, any of you. Not today. You've made your witness, and that's enough. Dost thou hear me, Susanna?"

"I hear thee," I said, and knew she was right.

She's a good soul, is Hester, and motherly — one of our people but not always at Meeting; she says someone must stay at home and out of trouble or how will life go on?

I left her in charge and went to the printer's and told Simon Race that John and Nat had been taken.

We stood talking with the works empty around us, the press silent.

"We must close the works down with the three of them gone," said Simon. "I can't run it alone."

"I could help thee."

He shook his head. "No. We'd need John, for the press. Besides, there's not much work coming in now from the town. I think people are nervous of being seen here."

He looked anxious, and I realized he had a child to support, and that if Mary's income dwindled, she might have to let him go, and me, too. Mary had given me my second month's pay early, knowing she might be arrested, and I had the weighty crown coin wrapped in a handkerchief and tucked under my mattress in the bed upstairs, where I hadn't slept for a week. It was time I went home, I thought, and found out how things were with my parents, and gave them the money. I needed none of it, for I still had spending money left from the two shillings I'd kept from my first pay.

That night I lay alone in the bed I had shared with Judith. Abigail slept nearby, and her brothers in the next room. But Judith was gone, and Nat; and Will — I dared not think about Will. I missed Mary, and wished I had her there to counsel me. But one thing I saw clearly: if we were to keep the meeting alive during this time of trouble, it must be the children who kept faith. And I was the eldest. I must be the one to lead them.

William

My father and I returned from Welshpool on Monday, having traveled most of the day. We had not gotten on well. He had kept me in the background during his business transactions, no doubt fearful that I would disgrace him as I had done with John Rhys. I was angry at being removed from Hemsbury and spoke only when spoken to. And although I was attentive to his commands, he complained that I was sullen.

It was late when we reached home, and both of us were hungry. I knew the servants would have a cold meal prepared that could be put on the table quickly, but I didn't want to wait. Ned came out to take the horses and help unload our packages, and while my father was engaged with him, I said, "I must go out.

I shall not be long," and was out of the courtyard and into the street before he could argue.

I went straight to the Mintons' shop. Hester opened the door and called Susanna, who came running. We flew into each other's arms.

"What news, love?" I asked.

"They are all taken," she told me. "Nat, Judith, John Pardoe, John and Isobel of the Seven Stars. All came before the mayor today and were sent to join the others in prison. They await trial at the sessions."

"It's finished, then? The meeting is closed down?"

"Only if we allow it. The children are free. We plan to keep the meeting. Will thou come? Say yes. I need thee there."

"And shall have me." I held her close. We would stand together as witnesses to the truth. "But with John and Isobel taken, how can we use the Seven Stars?"

"I have a key. And if they prevent us, we'll meet outside. The meeting is not illegal unless more than five people are over sixteen."

That pleased me. That would answer my father.

Before I went home, I walked for a while around the streets to get my courage up. I knew there could be no compromise with my father now. When I arrived back at the house I was trembling, keyed up for the conflict I knew must come.

Meriel met me in the hall. "Supper's ready, sir."

I thanked her, wondering if she could see how tense I was.

With my hat on, I made my way to the dining room. My heart was beating fast. Anne and our stepmother were just going in, and my father, also wearing his hat, was already there, about to take his place at the head of the table.

Anne looked up at me and whispered, "Will, your hat . . ." and then I saw her eyes widen in alarm as she realized what I was about to do.

My father, facing me across the room, understood at once. "Will," he said, and his voice was soft with menace, "take off your hat."

I stood still and took a breath. "I will not, Father."

He moved like lightning — up from his seat, down the length of the room — seized my hat, and flung it aside. He was red in the face and breathing heavily. The women stared, horrified, as I darted and retrieved my hat and went to put it back on, but he caught my arm and wrestled it away.

"I am the head of this household," he said, "and you will appear bareheaded before me or leave!"

My stepmother came between us, took the hat, and, with an angry glance at me, said, "Husband, don't distress yourself, I beg you. William, apologize to your father."

"I meant no offense, Father," I said.

"You meant to provoke me," he retorted, "and you succeeded. Will, I care nothing for your beliefs, if you call them that. But while you are in my house, you will give me respect."

"I do respect thee, Fa —"

But I got no farther, because he struck me such a blow across the face that I staggered back against the sideboard. Anne cried out, and Milly rushed into the room and began to bark, darting from one to another of us.

"Hush, Milly, hush!" said Anne while my stepmother took my father's arm and tried to persuade him to sit down. But nothing would stop him now; he began to beat me about the head and body with his fists while Anne screamed at him to stop and Milly barked and barked, and my stepmother closed the door as if that would prevent the servants from hearing.

I put up my arms to protect my face and endured the blows; I would not strike back. And part of me was imagining how funny the scene must look to an outsider, so that I found myself wanting to laugh and had to struggle to disguise it.

At last the women prevailed and my father was persuaded to sit down on condition that I left off my hat and never addressed him as "thee" again. I considered whether I should refuse this, and whether I should retrieve the hat, or let all be for now — and decided on the latter course. I was hungry and mentally exhausted, and felt sorry to have distressed them all so much.

So I stood until my father was seated, and then we all sat down, and Milly stopped yapping and settled under Anne's chair, and Meriel came in with the dishes as if she had overheard nothing.

We sat with heads bowed, my father gave thanks to God, and we ate, mostly in silence. My stepmother spoke solicitously to my father and cast reproachful looks at me, and Anne kept her attention on the dog, tossing scraps to her under the table.

Usually, my father and I would sit together and talk after supper, but that night he said he would go to his private room and read. My stepmother turned on me as he left, asking how I could behave so barbarously, as she put it, with my father tired from his travels; did I have no thought for his digestion? What sort of people had I been consorting with that would turn me against my own family?

"I have great love for my family, and always will," I said, and saw her flinch; for she knows that she is not family to me and never can be.

Later, in my room, I sat on the bed and covered my face with my hands and tried to clear my mind, but it was too full. I knew I had been churlish to my stepmother, not in what I said but in the way I had made her feel. I knew I had angered my father and that he could not understand the change in me. I looked around at the familiar room: the low chair that I'd used as a child now piled with books; the clothes chest carved with a scene of Adam and Eve and, coming between them, a serpent with a human face that used to frighten me; the four-poster bed with hangings embroidered long ago by my grandmother. This was my place. I belonged here, and I was jeopardizing it for a vision of life that could mean prison, punishment, even transportation to the colonies — Jamaica or Barbados.

I heard a faint knock at the door.

"Who is it?"

"Anne."

"Come in."

Her face, small under the elaborate arrangement of dark curls, looked pinched and tearful.

She came and sat beside me and put her arms around me, and I hugged her. She was rigidly corseted — much tighter-laced than Susanna — and could not bend from the waist, and it seemed to me that this was a denial of truth as much as hat-honor and deferential speech.

"I hate it when Father is angry with you," she said.

"It can't be helped, Anne."

"But why must you insult him by saying 'thee' and 'thou'?"

"It's not an insult. It puts us all on a level. I won't defer to anyone or expect anyone to defer to me. It makes us equal, as we are before God. Dost thou see?"

"No. I don't see why it matters; why you should upset everyone over it."

"I don't wish to, but . . . these outward forms are symbols. . . ." I struggled to explain, and ended, "It is the truth and I must act on it."

"Mother says Nicholas Barron will reject you as his apprentice and we shall all be shamed and Father's business will suffer. And she says there is a girl who has lured you into all this. Is there a girl, Will? Meriel says she's seen you going often into the Mintons', the glover's."

I felt a flash of anger. Mother says; Meriel says. They were all watching me.

"Is it true, Will?"

I said carefully, "There is a girl I like, but she has not lured me. I have been drawn to Quakers this long time past."

She focused on the girl. "Is it the glover's daughter? The tall, fair one?"

"No."

"Who, then?"

"Thou dost not know her."

"How old is she? Is she pretty?"

"I won't tell thee."

She got up then. "Well, you'd better be careful, if you want her kept secret. Mother says Father means to find out."

The following Thursday was the evening of the midsummer dinner. This feast is one of the big events of the civic year. The Council Chamber is set with long tables and decorated with flags and greenery, and all the councilors and aldermen and their wives and adult sons attend. I was invited this year for the first time. Anne was jealous; young girls were not invited.

"I'd gladly give thee my place," I said. "I've no wish to go and dress up and flaunt our father's wealth."

I was aware of sounding self-righteous, but the showiness of the feast went against all my instincts.

"I like you better dressed up," said Anne. "You look so drab since you met those Quakers. Where are your buttons with the silver embroidery?"

"In a pouch in my chamber. Thou may have them if thou wish."

"Father will not like your coat so plain."

"No." My father and stepmother and I had already had several arguments about what I should wear.

I had told him that I didn't want to go; that if I did go, I would be sure to distress him since I would wear simple clothes and not doff my hat to anyone.

"Nicholas Barron will be there," my father said. "He expects to see you. The last I heard, he was hoping to get the bond drawn up."

"He will have heard by now that I am not fit for his employ."

"You are in every way fit!" He sounded exasperated. "In upbringing, education, appearance, willingness to serve — or so it used to be. If only you would break free of these Quakers. . . . I insist that you come, Will. I could not explain your absence — unless you wish me to lie and say you are ill?"

He knew I would not want to be involved in a lie.

And so I joined them that evening: my father resplendent in gold and lace, my stepmother in a new green gown and with her hair bunched in curls at the sides, and myself in a dark blue coat with plain linen buttons and my hat with the gray plume firmly on my head.

It was a warm evening and the hall was full. There were strong mingled smells of perfume, flowers, herbs, and overheated bodies confined in layers of corsets and rich fabric. I felt hot, and saw that my stepmother's face was pink and shiny even before we began to greet people of our acquaintance.

"They have decked the hall beautifully!" she exclaimed, fanning herself.

I looked around at the flags in faded reds and golds, the flowers, the alcove decorated with greenery where musicians were arranging themselves with their instruments. The tables were laid with snowy linen and set with glass and silver; there were finger-bowls of rose-scented water and flowers all down the length. Anne would love this, I thought; she would enjoy every moment. And then I tried to imagine Susanna here, and could not.

Servants were busy setting out the food: dishes of beef, pork, and pheasant; a salmon, flaky soft and laid on a bed of dill; two entire swans, in pastry bases, arranged as if in life, with upraised wings; an array of pies and pastries and sauces; dishes of salad; vegetables cut into fancy shapes.

As everyone met and mingled, there was an outbreak of curtsying and bowing, and such a doffing of hats that it caused a welcome stir of air. I said good evening to people I knew and did not doff my hat, but my father suddenly snatched it from my head and thrust it into my hands, muttering, "Behave civilly for a few hours, and damn your principles, can't you?"

When we came to sit down, I found that I had been placed between my father and Nicholas Barron.

I felt hot and nervous, wondering how I should greet Barron without causing offense. But he took the initiative.

"Well, William, they're saying you've turned Quaker. Is it true?"

"Yes, s —" I had to struggle not to say "sir."

"And your father none too happy with it, I understand?"

I looked at my father, who was talking animatedly to someone across the table.

"It's the hat-honor and the way of speaking that anger him most."

"That's understandable," he said. He leaned back and regarded me. "Is it so important? Since it gives offense, why not abandon it? It is not the heart of your belief, surely?"

"No, indeed!" I began to tell him about the inward light, about waiting in the silence, about the spirit being accessible to everyone. He listened, apparently with interest, not interrupting as my father would. I like this man, I thought. I could serve him well, and make a success of my apprenticeship to him.

A servant came by and poured wine into each of our glasses. Barron took a few slices of beef, and indicated to me to take some. "So these outward signs . . . ? Tell me what they mean."

"We believe that the light of God is within every

man — and woman — so we do not recognize difference of rank."

"You don't? How would you address the king?"

"By his name: Charles Stuart."

"You don't consider the king above you in rank?"

"In worldly rank, yes. . . ." I felt that this conversation was becoming dangerous, and wished I had Sam Minton or Mary Faulkner to answer for me.

"If you were asked to take the oath of allegiance," he persisted, "would you take it?"

"No. But not because I deny allegiance to the Crown. Because I would not swear an oath — any oath."

He changed tack. "Of course, a more immediate problem is your intention to take part in illegal meetings."

"We deny that they *are* illegal."

"But the law says otherwise, and people have been imprisoned. Will you defy the law?"

"If I must."

"You are very young to take on so much, so quickly."

"I have been thinking of these things for some time."

The dishes were being passed around, and we helped ourselves to salmon and some small pies containing spicy meat. Nicholas Barron began, to my relief, to tell me about his business and the work his previous apprentice had taken on. He described his new premises in London, their nearness to the docks, the convenience, the extra space, the contacts with merchants from all over Europe. I knew it was work that I could take in my stride, that would challenge and interest me. I knew, too, that he'd keep me in good style and pay me a wage. And I would travel: to Belgium, France, Italy.

The wineglasses were refilled, and I grew more relaxed. My father introduced me to another alderman and we talked awhile, and then I listened to the musicians.

Much later, when the dinner was over and people were leaving, Nicholas Barron drew me aside.

"You know, I'd like to take you on as my apprentice," he said. "You have the manner and the education, and you are a youth I could work with and who would be a help in my business. You will stand up for your principles, too, and I admire that. But, to be blunt, Will, I need a lad who can stay out of prison. I think I can trust you not to cheat or drink or fight or otherwise get into trouble, but the laws are tightening against Quakers. The London Quakers are numerous and troublesome and the law comes down heavily on them. Soon the only way for a Quaker to worship in peace will be for him to do it secretly, or in a very small group. If you attend meetings, you'll be arrested, and I don't want to spend my time and money bailing you out."

"I can't promise — " I began.

"Don't promise anything. Think about it. It will be a few weeks before I need your decision. There's another youth I could ask, but I'd prefer you. Consider whether you might compromise, Will. For my part, I believe the act's a bad one and will only make more Quakers; people flourish under adversity. But I don't make the laws. Think about it. I've spoken to your father. He knows how I feel."

And then he was gone, before I could gather my answer. I knew, of course, that I must turn down his offer. I could not compromise; I could not put God aside to further my career.

But I also knew my father would be furious.

We argued half the night.

"He has made you an offer that's more than reasonable," my father said. "You will write to him tomorrow and accept."

He was red-faced, flushed with wine.

My stepmother tried to calm him. "Husband, come to bed. It's late, and you spoil a pleasant evening. Will, tell your father you will think about it tomorrow."

"He knows I will not."

"And what else do you intend to do with yourself, sirrah?" demanded my father. "Will you live here, idle, at my expense?"

"I mean to look for work," I said stiffly. But I felt shamed, knowing that he was in the right and should not have to keep me. I should leave his house. But to go where? Without work, I could pay no rent.

"You need not think I'll come up with the money for any other bond you choose," he said. "If you tie yourself to a Quaker master, you'll get nothing from me. Let *them* look after you — I cast you off! We'll see how long your principles last then."

My stepmother said, "Will has been given time to consider the offer. Let him sleep on it, at least."

Finally she persuaded my father to his bed, and I went to mine. But not to sleep. I lay awake with a pounding headache, and relived the conversation I'd had with Nicholas Barron over and over again.

There was another thing on my mind that Nicholas Barron as yet did not know about: if I accepted his offer, it would take me far away from Susanna. Unless . . . And then I realized something else. When an apprentice signs a bond, he agrees to certain conditions. One of them is that he shall not marry during the seven-year term of his apprenticeship.

Susanna

"I have scarcely seen thee this week."

Will and I were in the bookshop, snatching a moment together. The day was hot, and even with the counters down and the shop door wide I felt sticky and uncomfortable. There was a film of sweat on Will's forehead.

He had told me about Nicholas Barron's offer, and that he intended to reject it, and I felt a mixture of joy and guilt — but mostly joy, because I had dreaded his going away to London. And yet even if he stayed here, we were not free; he could not acknowledge me.

"I daren't go to the Mintons' too often," he said. "Anne says the servants have noticed. I don't want to lead my father to thee."

I longed to be alone with him, away from Hemsbury.

Sometimes, in my imagination, I took the two of us to Long Aston, to a field I knew that sloped down toward woodland and a little stream. We walked hand in hand through the green corn, and when we reached the edge of the wood, we found a place away from the track and lay down together on rough grass and leaves, and heard a cuckoo calling in the wood, and the murmur of the stream. We were quite alone. No one came to disturb us; no eyes watched. There was a scent of honeysuckle and dry earth, and Will's face above mine was dusted with pollen. I put my arms around his neck and kissed him.

I felt shame when I dared to imagine more. Will and I were not promised in marriage; he had never spoken of it. He was forbidden to me, and I knew I should not be thinking of him in that way.

And yet I kept the picture of that woodland place in mind while I went about my work. The cesspit in the cellar stank and the streets were foul with rubbish. I saw a dead cat, bloated and buzzing with flies, on Broad Street, and butchers' waste clogging the gutters. Hemsbury folk fear plague in hot weather. Hester told me to carry a posy of herbs to ward off infection; she made me one from the

Mintons' garden, and I felt safer having it about me.

One blessing of the hot weather was that the laundry dried quickly. There was much to do, for we struggled to help our friends in prison keep clean. Judith had her monthly courses that week, and I took home her bloodstained rags and put them to soak in a pail of water, then washed them and spread them on the bushes to bleach in the sunshine. On fifth-day Hester and I washed a pile of shirts and shifts, helped by Abigail. We knew that the prisoners would come to court soon and we did not want them to appear like vagabonds.

On seventh-day we filled a basket with clean clothes, rags, and bunches of thyme and rosemary, and went to the prison.

The smell, as we went down into the dungeons, almost drove me back. God give them strength to endure it, I thought. And I dreaded to see how my friends might look.

We heard someone speaking in a loud voice.

"They rant on, those Quakers," the jailer grumbled. The heavy wooden door had a grille in it, high up. He looked in, called, "Visitors!" and opened up.

Hester and I went in. As he locked the door behind us, we were swallowed up in the buzz of voices, the press of stinking, unwashed bodies, the smells of excrement, blood, and vomit.

I felt as if caught in a trap. I could scarcely endure this for one moment, and yet they were here day and night.

I saw Judith first. My friend, who had been so fresh and fair, was changed: her skin grayish, her hair hanging loose under a dirty cap, flea bites on her neck and arms. When she saw me, she struggled to hold back tears.

"Judith!"

We squeezed our way toward each other and embraced. I felt myself wanting to cry with her, but that would not help.

She drew back, smearing a hand across her face, and I noticed with repulsion that there was dirt under her fingernails and ingrained in the skin of her hands. "I never was made for this, Su," she said. "We are so crowded that only half of us can lie down at one time. My mother is ill. She burns with fever. Many are the same — fainting and feverish. . . ."

"Jail fever?"

"We fear so. There is so much filth, and we can't wash; we have lice and fleas." She shuddered. "I know I should be stronger. I think of Dan; he's still manacled in the Pit. Oh, but yesterday someone puked near me and it splashed all down my gown and I can't get rid of the smell."

"We've brought clean linen," I said, glad to have something practical to offer. "And thou can have my skirt." I was stepping out of it as I spoke, for it seemed to me far more important that Judith should be comfortable than that I should not be seen by men in my shift; so much had our lives changed. "I'll take thine and clean it. Here. It might be a little short."

"No matter. Oh, Su!" And she started to laugh, and soon we were both laughing.

"Wait!" I said. I went to the basket and brought out a clean cap of hers, and a shift, and a parcel of rags for her courses.

"Thou givst me courage," she said, becoming grave again.

I stepped into her skirt, and rolled it over at the waist to shorten it. The women went into a huddle, changed into their clean linen, and put the dirty clothes in our basket for washing.

I found Nat in better spirits than Judith, though just as dirty. But he had lost his jaunty grin and looked leaner and more sober than I had seen him before. Mary remained strong. She was thin and gaunt, but she brushed aside my questions about her health.

"What news?" she asked me. "Hast thou heard from thy parents? From Eaton Bellamy Meeting?"

"No. But our people are being arrested all around. A packman came the other day with messages. Brentbridge jail is full. And they say there are many arrested at Ludlow and Hereford and Birmingham."

"And my shop?"

"Simon manages alone. I'm living at the Mintons'. The print room has closed."

She nodded. "Tell Simon not to fear for his wages. I have money put by."

"The meeting . . ." I wanted to cheer her. "We shall keep the meeting. The children will keep it as long as we must. And Will says he'll come."

She looked at me with concern. "Don't persuade Will into trouble."

"I don't! He chooses to come."

"They'll deal harshly with you all," she warned. "They won't spare any, even the little ones."

It was midafternoon when Hester and I returned to the Mintons'. High Street was busy, for it was cattle market day and the town full of country people. As we approached the shop, I saw two children in home-spun clothes stop and look up at the glover's sign — and my heart leaped in joy and alarm.

"Deb!" I shouted. "Isaac!" I turned to Hester. "It's my brother and sister!"

I gave my basket to Hester and ran toward them. We came together in a huddle on the street, and I felt tears rising as I exclaimed, "How did you get here? Are Mam and Dad arrested? Oh, Isaac, Deb, I'm so glad to see you!"

Deb hugged me as I dropped down beside her, and Isaac said, "We went to Mary Faulkner's, but the man said Mary was in prison and thou gone to the Mintons'. So we came here. . . . Deb's tired."

"She didn't walk all the way?"

"No. A farmer brought us into town in his cart."

"And Mam and Dad?" I asked. I knew they must have been taken.

"Arrested — both of them. On first-day. They are in prison at Norton. Eaton Bellamy Meeting is almost all there."

Hester had caught up to me. "Bring the children inside, Susanna," she said. "I'll fetch food and drink. Dost thou like milk, my poppet?"

Deb nodded, and put her thumb in her mouth. "Goody Allen's geese frighted me," she said into my shoulder.

I stood up and led her indoors as Isaac explained. "Innkeeper Allen and his wife would have taken us in. Said we could stay as long as need be, and I could help out back for our keep. But Deb cried a lot so I said we'd go to thee. Their son — that was him in the cart — was going to town, and he took us all the way. We were quite merry till we reached Faulkner's and found thee gone. . . ." His chin wobbled.

I put my arms around him. "Well, you are with me now. You did right to come. We'll send a message to Mam and Dad, to say you are both safe here."

But to myself I wondered how I was going to care for them, with all our friends in prison and even my work and wages uncertain.

William

"You will come to church tomorrow," my father said on Saturday night.

"I will not."

We had been sparring for two days, since the evening of the civic dinner. I had refused to write and accept Nicholas Barron's offer, but had made several attempts to write a letter of rejection that would not offend — each time crumpling up the paper in frustration and throwing it into the fireplace. I stalked about the house in my hat, refusing to go bareheaded before my father, and used "thee" and "thou" whenever I spoke at all. He did not attack me again, but banished me to the kitchen at mealtimes, saying I could eat with the servants if I would not remove my hat.

The servants were puzzled but sympathetic. As I

sat with them I became aware, for the first time, of their lives. Joan disliked Rebecca, my stepmother's maidservant, and the two sniped at each other continually. Ned spoke to me of his time in the army. I hadn't known Ned had been a soldier, never thought much about these people I'd lived with for years. Meriel, it seemed, had a lover — a draper's servant — who appeared at the back door on Saturday evening and was alarmed to find me there.

Meriel slipped outside with him into the warm dusk.

"Don't tell Mistress," said Joan. "The girl needs a bit of life."

On Sunday — first-day — morning I did not wait for confrontation. I was out of bed and down to the kitchen before even the servants were awake. I drank some beer, then took a chunk of bread from the crock and went out the way Meriel had gone.

The town was quiet: a housewife was mopping her step, a girl walking with a yoke of pails to the conduit. The Mintons' shutters were closed; I could not call there at this hour. I went down to the riverside and sat on a wall eating the bread. Then I closed my eyes and tried to clear my mind and make space for the light. When the streets began to stir with people, I went to Cross Street.

Susanna was there, in the yard of the Seven Stars,

and with her the Minton boys, Tom and Joe, and perhaps a dozen other children. A little one of four or five was holding her hand.

Her face showed love and relief when she saw me, but she said only, "I'm glad thou'rt here, Will." She glanced down at the little girl. "This is my sister, Deborah."

I remembered the child then. "We've met before," I said to her. But Deborah hid her face in Susanna's skirts.

I looked at Susanna. "Thy parents? Are they arrested?"

"Yes. The children came yesterday. Isaac is over there."

He was like her: slight build, golden-brown hair. I knew him to be about twelve years old.

I saw that I was the only person over sixteen. I counted eight boys and five girls between about nine and fifteen years, and little Deborah. We were not an illegal meeting under the terms of the act since there were not five adults present.

"I doubt the authorities will trouble us," I said, and felt almost disappointed; I was keyed up for conflict.

"Oh, they will," said Susanna. "They will come."

She let us in with the Mintons' key. The seats were in some disarray, a few toppled over — unchanged, I supposed, since the last meeting had been broken up.

We set them upright, and Susanna and Tom and I sat down. Isaac and Deborah sat either side of Susanna, but the other children all went to their usual places scattered around the room, some at the back.

Susanna looked around at them. "Come nearer," she said. "We should all sit together."

Gradually they moved forward, and we formed a half-circle.

The children fell quiet at once, even those I'd seen fidget and play during Meeting. A new seriousness seemed to have come upon them. I saw that Susanna was nervous; her hands were clenched tight. I tried to relax into the silence and seek the Lord's will on how we might respond if the militia came.

But we had no time to find the silence. We were only a few minutes into the meeting when the door burst open.

I looked up, my heart thumping, expecting to see soldiers, led by the sheriff. But only one man came into the room: my father.

Susanna

J guessed at once who the man was. Will gave a small moan at sight of him, and rose to his feet.

"Stay there," he said to me. And to the man: "Father, you should not have come here —"

His father was ablaze with anger. "Get out!" he shouted. "You are expected in church."

He seized Will by the arm and tried to drag him away, but Will resisted. "I won't go. Father! Calm yourself. This is a religious meeting. We have come here to worship —"

"Worship?" His glance flicked contemptuously over our group. "A rabble of children? With no minister present?"

I stood up then, and faced him; took a breath to steady myself. "God is here," I said.

He looked at me, and I returned his stare. I saw in his eyes the moment of recognition when he realized who I must be. His expression hardened.

"You bold-faced little whore!" he said. "What have you done to my son?"

I felt shock, as if he had punched me, and took a step back. At the same moment Will sprang forward, and Tom jumped up to try to make peace. Deb, seeing me distressed, began to wail. Then I heard men's voices outside, and in through the open doorway came Robert Danson, followed by several constables.

Danson was stopped in his tracks at sight of Will's father. "Mr. Heywood. . . ." he said, uncertainly.

Henry Heywood was breathing fast. "I am here to retrieve my son from this gathering," he said.

Danson recovered himself, took charge, and declared the meeting illegal. Will at once spoke up and said that he was the only person over sixteen years old and so it was lawful. But Danson retorted, "This is clearly a riotous and tumultuous meeting, a danger to the public peace. It is therefore an unlawful assembly." He turned to Henry Heywood. "Take your son home, sir." And to the constables: "Drive them out. If they will not move, beat them."

The children were courageous. None of them moved. Will's father tried to wrestle him toward the door. At a signal from Danson, the constables set about the rest of us with rods, striking out even at the youngest children, so that all were forced to get up.

I crouched to protect Deb, angry with myself for having brought her into danger. A blow from a rod caught me on the shoulder. I cried out, and saw Will struggling in vain to reach us, held back by his father and Danson. All around me children were scrambling to get out, arms raised to ward off the blows.

I am the eldest, I thought; I brought this meeting about; I must take charge, as Mary would. I turned to the constables, my arms shielding Deb, and said, "You need not beat us! We are leaving."

Once outside, they herded us together. I guessed we appeared a sorry little group, and I drew myself up and held Robert Danson's gaze. Will and his father were arguing, both red in the face. Will moved forward to join us, but the constables barred his way.

"Go home with your father, Master Heywood," said Danson. "I shall not arrest you."

And Will had no choice but to go. I saw the shame in his eyes as he looked back at me.

Now Danson demanded the key to the meeting room. I gave it to him, and he locked the door and kept the key.

"You will not meet here again," he said. He turned to the constables. "Take them to Bridewell. A night there will teach them obedience."

I felt a moment of panic. I had not expected this. The Bridewell is a workhouse for the rough sort. There they lock up vagabonds and vagrants, brawling apprentices, those the worse for drink, and loose women.

Abigail looked at me, wide-eyed and scared.

"Don't be afraid," I said. "We shall all be together. And it's only for one night."

But I did not feel brave.

The constables rounded us up quickly and marched us there. Deb came, too, because they could not pry her from my side.

When we arrived, the older boys, including Isaac, were taken away to join a gang of men breaking stones. The rest of us were set to picking oakum: old frayed rope that had to be unraveled to make fibrous stuff for packaging. After a few hours my back ached and my fingers were bleeding. There was a vagrant woman there with matted hair, skin like old creased leather, and a ripe stink about her. She seemed a little mad, but was kind; showed us how to do the work and defended Abigail from the overseer when the fellow accused her of slacking. I saw the light burning strong within her and told her so.

She cackled. "I live on the road. Only light I know is sun or moon."

"The light of Christ is within you," I said.

She looked me over. "I seen those Quaker women," she said, "after the war. Tramping the roads, preaching. Saw one whipped and the branks put over her head to quiet her. Broke her jaw. You should stay home, wench, and spin. Earn yourself a husband — eh?"

At the end of the day, the boys were released from the stone-breaking and came stiffly indoors. We lay on filthy straw and heard rats squeaking. Deb whimpered with fear. I held her close and soothed her till she fell asleep.

For myself, my thoughts kept me awake. I saw again, over and over, Henry Heywood's look of hatred for me, and heard his words. Every time I remembered it I found myself trembling and tearful with shock; I had never been so much hated before.

I tried to still my thoughts and wait on the Lord, but the stillness would not come. I thought about Will, imagined how he must be feeling now, after being shamed in front of me, taken home like a child. I wanted to put my arms around him, reassure him, tell him I did not think any the less of him, that I loved him. Henry Heywood believed it was because of me that Will was here, but I knew it was not; I knew he had found his own way to the light.

And yet I *did* feel guilt. I'd been glad when Will told me he would turn down Nicholas Barron's offer. This offer, if he took it up, and went to London, could make him one day a rich man, perhaps influential in society. Here, with me, there could be nothing but persecution and trouble. And love, my heart insisted: and love. If he married me, if we were together, and lived in the truth and loved each other well, no trouble would be beyond bearing.

"You bold-faced little whore," his father had called me. Henry Heywood would exert all his power to keep us apart. But I had power, too, and would use it.

William

All the way home, my father blustered and shouted at me, so angry that he seemed not to notice the stares of passersby.

"I forbade you to go to that place!"

"And I said I would!"

"You won't go again. I'll lock you up."

"You can't keep me in."

"It's that girl, isn't it? That bold wench? She's the cause of this. They set these girls on to entice men."

"She did not entice me!" I was still furious at the way he had insulted Susanna. "I pursued *her*! She is a maid of fifteen and knows nothing of enticement."

"Huh! They know, these country girls."

We had reached the house, and the servants must have heard us as we quarreled our way across the yard.

My stepmother and sister were waiting — dressed in their finery, I noted angrily, as if the church was a place to parade wealth.

"We are too late for church now," said my stepmother, with a reproachful look at me.

"But I have hauled him out, as I said I would." My father pushed me in ahead of him and snatched the hat from my head. "He has a girl — that's the cause of it all. Some little drab of a maidservant, by the look of her."

"I know the one," said my stepmother. "She lodges with the glover's family."

"Find out her name. I'll bring a complaint against her, get her sent back to her village."

They were talking about me as if I were not there. I could not tolerate any more.

"Her name is Susanna Thorn," I said. "She's a weaver's daughter, from Long Aston. And I love her and intend to marry her."

There was a moment's silence. Then my father gave a snort of laughter. "*Marry?* You are my only son, the heir to my business, and you intend to marry that girl? You must have lost your wits entirely."

We spoke no more about the matter that day. Indeed, we spoke little at all. I ate in the kitchen, where Joan was kind and asked no questions. Anne, I guessed, had been instructed by our stepmother not to talk to me about Susanna, but whenever we met, she showed me her allegiance with looks of sympathy.

I had not meant to tell my father I would marry Susanna. I had thought about marriage, felt it might happen, but had not spoken of it to anyone, not even to her. Now that the words were spoken, it became a thing of substance, a commitment. There was a sense of rightness about it, and I became desperate to see Susanna, to ask her, to be sure she would have me.

I planned to slip out after supper, but before I could do so, Ned came to me with a message from the Mintons' servant, Hester, saying that Susanna and all the children had been sent to Bridewell and would be kept in overnight.

"Bridewell!" I stared at Ned. I could not bear to think of Susanna in that place while I slept comfortably at home.

Ned tried to cheer me. "It's not so bad, sir, the Bridewell. I've been in there myself, time past. And they'll be out in the morning."

"I should have been there with them," I said.

I took the stairs at a run, intending to confront my father and demand that he get them all released. But by the time I reached the drawing-room door, I had thought better of it. He would not help;

nothing could be done tonight; and to insist on it would only turn his anger even more against Susanna. I went to my room and lay awake much of the night, knowing that she, too, must be awake and thinking of me.

The next day the Quakers who were held in prison were brought to trial.

My father made no objection when I said I would go to the courthouse — indeed he thought it would be a lesson for me — but he insisted that I sit with him at the front, among the town councilors.

We arrived early, but already the building was packed. It was clear that most of the spectators were townsfolk, but many others looked like Quakers, and I realized that they must have come from miles around to support their friends. The benches were full; people were standing and many wore hats that blocked the view. The weather was still hot and the doors and windows had been thrown open, but still the smell and press of people were overwhelming.

I felt a rush of relief when I saw Susanna there, already freed from the Bridewell. She was at the far side, near the front, with Tom Minton. They were standing. She looked around once and saw me, but with my father beside me I could only acknowledge her with a discreet nod.

There was a stir as the jury began taking their places. I saw Susanna and the families of those accused scanning the faces of these men. Would they make up their own minds, I wondered, or would they be intimidated by the justices? I knew there could sometimes be trouble for juries if they came up with a verdict the judges did not like. They were all citizens of the town: merchants, shopkeepers, and the like. Some I knew by sight.

A hush fell as the justices came in. One was Sir William Cheevers, known for his rigor against Dissenters. He was an old man, tall and upright, with a long, lean, supercilious face, full of the confidence that comes with power. The other was Richard Stourton, a heavy, red-faced, choleric-looking fellow. Neither of them, I imagined, would have any sympathy for Quakers.

As the first prisoner was about to be called, I saw a clerk approach the mayor, and some consultation between him and two of the aldermen; and then a message was passed to the justices, who conferred briefly. Justice Cheevers's face clouded and I thought I caught the word "coroner."

"What is it?" I whispered to my father. But he did not know.

Before we could learn more, the first prisoner was called.

"Daniel Kite!"

He appeared wild as ever, auburn curls springing from beneath his tall black hat. But when I looked closer, I saw that he had lost weight and there were dark circles under his eyes. I knew he had been confined in the Pit for so-called troublemaking, and his suffering showed, but the spirit was still strong in him.

"Take off your hat, sirrah!" demanded Justice Cheevers.

Daniel turned to him. "By what law dost thou command me to do so?"

A buzz of pleasure and expectation went around the court and people settled to enjoy the exchange.

"You do not prosper your case by this behavior," began Cheevers.

"I only ask by what law —"

"We are ministers of justice. We represent the king's person. Therefore you should pay due reverence to our authority."

Daniel seemed to consider this. "I don't keep my hat on in contempt of the king," he said, "or in contempt of any authority. But why choose my hat? Why not some other garment?"

And he glanced down at his body as if considering what else he might remove. This caused an outbreak of laughter — the more so, perhaps, because he was comely and people remembered that he was the man who had walked almost naked through the market-place two months before. I saw some of the Quakers shaking their heads as if to say "He goes too far," but others were smiling; and the townsfolk loved it.

The justices, however, did not.

"Take his hat from him!" commanded Cheevers. "And make sure the other prisoners are hatless before they appear."

An usher seized the hat — nervously, for Daniel was a well-muscled man, a blacksmith by trade. As Daniel moved, one of his sleeves slipped back and I saw red scabs and bruising on his wrist. I remembered then that they had kept him manacled in prison. He did not resist the usher, only remarking loudly as the hat was taken, "Reverence and respect are not shown by removing the hat, or any other part of the clothing."

For this he was fined five pounds, to be added to any other fine he might incur — for the proceedings against him had not yet begun.

A witness — one of the soldiers — was brought in to testify that he had seen the accused at an unlawful meeting held under the pretense of a religious exercise, that this religious exercise was conducted in a manner other than that allowed by the Liturgy of the Church of England, and that he was seen there with other malefactors to the terror of the people and disturbance of the peace.

At this last, sighs of exasperation and even laughter went around the room. Yet underlying them I heard a murmur; there was genuine fear in the town of unruly Dissenters.

Justice Cheevers called for silence.

"Daniel Kite, what do you say to these charges?"

"I say the evidence does not prove me guilty of being at an unlawful meeting."

I saw that the judge was growing impatient. "Were you *there*?" he demanded. "At that time and at that place? If you were, the law judges the meeting to have been unlawful."

"The meeting was simply a meeting," said Daniel. "The unlawfulness of it must be proved by something done or said." And he turned to the jury. "Take notice, jurymen, that the witness has not proved that anything occurred at this meeting to make it unlawful."

Now the justices had had enough.

"*We* will direct the jury's attention," said Cheevers. "Take the prisoner away."

I saw that some of the Quakers in the courtroom were taking notes.

The next prisoner was the tanner I had sat next to at my first meeting. He did not attempt to argue, but cried out, "You are like the scribes and Pharisees! They said they had a law, and by that law they crucified the Lord of Life!"

A roar went up from the room. I saw Cheevers's face harden. He spoke harshly. "Send him down."

They called Mary Faulkner next. She knew the law.

"I am here indicted for being at an unlawful meeting," she said, "but it is not yet proved that the meeting *was* unlawful."

She stood challenging the judges, her stance aggressive, like a man's, her voice and mind keen; and I saw how threatening and unwomanly they must find her.

Stourton snapped, "It was held under a pretense of worshiping God and contrary to the Liturgy of the Church of England."

"But if there is no pretense? If we truly meet to worship God, must we suffer for that?"

Stourton, red-faced, cried, "Yes, you must!" and people in the room drew breath in shock and dismay. The Quaker note-takers scribbled.

I saw that Justice Cheevers was annoyed at Stourton's rash remark. He intervened. "You are not indicted for worshiping God, but for being at an unlawful assembly."

"Where no unlawful thing was done or said?"

"We don't care what you did there. We have proved that you did meet."

Mary gave him a look almost of pity. "You are executing a law which is contrary to the Law of God."

"Take her away."

Someone behind me murmured, "It's a farce. A show. Why do they try them?"

As the morning wore on, I felt the mood in the courtroom vary as different people testified. The townsfolk had not liked Mary. For all her common sense, it was her unwomanly manner that repelled them. I heard snatches of talk around me: "They deny the Church . . . lead young people away from authority. . . ." "We'll have riots. . . ." I felt frustrated by their lack of understanding. Couldn't they see the honesty of the prisoners? Couldn't they feel the spirit at work in the courtroom? A group near the back began to cheer every time a prisoner was sent down, but gradually, as one testimony after another was made, there was some sympathy, too, and admiration. As for me, I felt myself strengthened and uplifted. If others could be steadfast, so could I. I saw Nicholas Barron's offer for the temptation it was. I'd have fine clothes, prestige, the prospect of a good career, a comfortable life — but the life of the spirit was here, in this courtroom.

Fewer than half the prisoners were seen that day. The rest would come tomorrow.

The last to be called was Alice Betts, a shoemaker's wife and a simple woman with no skill in argument. But her testimony reached me like no other. She said, "I know nothing of your law, but I have often met among the dear children of the Lord. And if God grant me life and strength to do so, I shall meet with them again and again."

She was sent away, and the jury went out, Stourton calling after them, "You'll get no dinner till we have a right verdict!"

Despite this, they took half an hour, and I wondered whether any had been wrestling with their consciences in that time. They pronounced all the prisoners guilty. The judges sighed in satisfaction, stood up, and thanked the jury for their good service. Then Cheevers delivered the sentence: all were to be fined five pounds, and must remain in prison for three months with hard labor or until their fines be paid. And he warned them that if they offended again, they would be fined ten pounds with six months' hard labor, and that for a third offense they would face transportation to the colonies of the New World for seven years.

And then the court adjourned for the day.

I left with my father. He signaled to me to come with him as the aldermen began moving out of the court-room. They were going to share a meal at the Bull.

In the tavern all kept their hats on and I was not conspicuous, though I knew there had been plenty of talk about me and I caught some councilors looking me over for signs of dissent.

They were talking, not of the sentences, which I suppose were as expected, but of that interruption I had noticed at the beginning of the proceedings, when the coroner was mentioned.

"There has been an outbreak of jail fever," my father explained to me. "Two of the prisoners died early this morning —"

"Died! Who?"

I thought of Nat and Judith. I had not seen them.

He shrugged. "I forget."

"Judith Minton? Nathaniel Lacon?"

"Neither of those." I gave thanks in silence as he continued. "Several more are too sick to come to court. No one wants them there for fear of contagion. And now the coroner's involved. He's sure to com-plain about the overcrowding. But where else can they be put?"

He spoke as if the dying people were nothing but

an administrative nuisance. And yet I knew he was not a heartless man. I remembered when a young servant we once had was ill, how he paid for the apothecary, took all care, and was brought to tears when, despite everything, the lad died.

"Perhaps they should go home," I said.

He looked at me sharply. "If they want to go home, there are several of them who could afford to pay their fines. But you may be sure they'll choose to make martyrs of themselves."

Alderman Green leaned across. "We'll have to move some of them to the Stonegate, or the Bridewell."

"The Bridewell's not suitable," my father said.

"But if we fill up the Stonegate, where will we put the felons?"

I said, without thinking, "You admit the Quakers are not felons, then?"

Both men glared at me for my impertinence. At once I felt admonished, and rightly so. It was bred into me not to speak disrespectfully to an older person. But even as I apologized and sat with head bowed, I reflected that Daniel Kite would not have been quelled so easily. Somehow, I felt, there must be a way of combining respect for elders with my own integrity.

As expected, the coroner pronounced himself shocked by conditions at the Castlegate prison and warned of the spread of disease. Half the prisoners were to be moved immediately to the Stonegate.

To my surprise, I saw them that afternoon as I looked out of my bedroom window. They were walking along High Street in a group — about twenty of them — but with no guards visible. People were staring. I heard George Woodall, the tailor, call out, "Make a run for it! Now! You have your chance!"

The Quakers acknowledged him but shook their heads.

I saw Daniel Kite, and Judith beside him, and ran downstairs and out into the street to speak to them. Both looked thin, but in good spirits. Susanna had told me that they loved each other, and I guessed that suffering together had helped to strengthen the bond between them.

"We are all going to the Stonegate," Daniel said, "across town. The constables said we might take ourselves there, since they know we won't try to escape."

I wished them courage, and left them.

It was late that evening, after supper, that I slipped out again and hurried to the Mintons' house, intent on seeing Susanna.

Tom answered the door, with Abigail hovering behind him, but when I asked for Susanna, they told me she was not there.

Susanna

$\mathcal{I}$n the early evening of the day our friends appeared in court, there came a knocking at the Mintons' shop door.

Hester and I were preparing supper. She stopped work and went downstairs. I heard a boy's voice, urgent, then Hester's panting breath as she hurried back up.

At once I was alarmed. I ran to the top of the stairs, where the children were already gathering.

"A message from the prison," Hester said. "Nat Lacon is ill with jail fever, and cannot stand. He's to be released, and Mary Faulkner with him. Thou'll be needed, Susanna."

"I'll go at once."

"And I'll come with thee; help prepare the sick-room."

Quickly we made arrangements.

I told Isaac to take care of Deb and on no account to come to Mary's house, for fear of contagion. "And tell Will." I turned to Tom and Abigail. "If Will comes here, don't let him follow me. He must stay away. You'll tell him?"

They promised. "And I'll look after Deb," said Abigail.

As we hurried downstairs, Hester said, "Mary fears for the lad's life. She's sent for Simon Race to bring the money for their release and says she will nurse Nat herself. The fever has taken hold at the Castlegate. Two more died this afternoon, but the boy could not give me names. . . . Hast thou herbs back there? Feverfew? And rosemary? There's plenty in our garden. . . ."

Her voice ran on, but all I could think was that Nat was ill and might die. The horror of it was like a cold pit opening at my feet.

When we reached the shop on Broad Street, we found it closed. Simon must already have gone to the prison. Hester set about laying a fire in the kitchen while I took a broom and a dust cloth and went up to Nat's room.

The cleaning had been neglected of late, with so

much happening and Mary not around to remind me of my duties. I knocked down cobwebs, dusted the bed hangings and the chair and washstand, and swept the floor.

All the time I was thinking, selfishly, not of Nat, but of Will. I had not seen him since we were separated on first-day. And now it would be a week or more before we could meet, and who knew but that Mary might also be carrying the sickness. Common sense told me that *I* was in danger, that I could sicken and die within days. I'd seen it happen to a young girl at the farm where I'd worked last year; a strong young lass, fit and cheerful at evening milking, sickened the next day, and dead before the week was out. But I did not believe I could die; I felt so much alive. All my fear was for Will, who had been in court, close to prisoners who might at any time collapse with the fever. If Will fell sick and died, I thought, *then* I should die.

Hester came puffing upstairs. "Water's heating," she said.

A large wooden chest on the landing held all the sheets and pillow covers and towels, stored between layers of lavender. Together we made up the bed with clean sheets, then closed the windows and drew the curtains. Hester brought towels and a wash ball scented with sage and laid them ready.

When the kitchen fire was well alight, I put some red-hot embers in a metal dish and took it upstairs and burned rosemary in the room to clean the air. The smoky scent was strong and comforting.

Soon we heard them coming.

They brought Nat home on a pallet, Simon and a neighbor holding either end and trying not to jolt him as they hurried over the cobbles. Mary walked alongside, and as they came in through the side door, I thought she looked weak and pale. But the sight of Nat shocked me. He was burning hot, tossing from side to side, and crying out words that made no sense. He seemed not to know any of us. I looked at him with pity and terror, and silently begged his forgiveness, and God's, for having thought more of Will's safety when it was Nat who needed my care.

Mary led the way upstairs and I followed with a bowl of warm water, which I placed on the washstand.

"Leave me with him," Mary said. She was panting and grasped the rail as she reached the top of the stairs.

"Thou'rt sick, too," I said.

"No. It's jail weakness only — we all had it — and lack of sleep."

"I'll help thee. Hester is making a draft of feverfew."

I laid a spare sheet over the bed and the men gently lifted Nat and placed him on it and then withdrew downstairs. Nat was dirty from lying on the prison floor. Bits of mucky straw clung to his hair and clothes, and his face had a shining film of grime. Mary dampened a cloth and wiped his face and began picking out dirt and lice from his hair. Nat moaned and flung himself from side to side. Suddenly he reared up, shouting, "They're here! They're here!" and tried to stand. It took the two of us to hold him down, and I felt a terrifying strength in him. His eyes glittered and he stared at an empty corner of the room. "Here! All! They're here — see!"

He stared so fixedly at the empty space that I felt the hairs rise on the back of my neck. When his gaze switched to me, I could endure no more and cried out in terror, "He's possessed!"

But Mary pushed him gently down, soothed him, and said, "Never fear. Never fear." I was not sure if she was talking to him or to both of us. But then she looked at me and said, "God is over all. No demons can hurt thee."

"But he — something is here . . . in the room," I whimpered.

"It can't hurt thee," Mary repeated. She turned

practical, nodded toward Nat's clothes chest. "Fetch a clean nightshirt. If we can get him out of these foul clothes, it will be better for him."

It took all my courage to cross the room. With the curtains drawn, it was shadowy, and I sensed the presence of unholy things in every darkened space, every fold of cloth. Nat continued to moan and jabber. But Mary was waiting. I opened the lid, thanked God a nightshirt lay on top and I need not rummage, and closed the chest quickly.

By this time Mary had gotten Nat's shirt off. "Help me with these breeches and stockings," she said.

His skin was hot like fire to the touch, and I saw a faint red rash rising all over his body. I had never been close to a naked man before, except my brother when he was little, and despite my fear I looked with interest, and thought of Will and imagined him naked, and then felt ashamed for having done so; I was relieved when we had Nat covered to the knees in the nightshirt. Mary helped me pull out the soiled sheet, and I busied myself making a bundle of it with Nat's dirty clothes and took it out to the landing to await fumigation and washing.

Hester came up at that moment with a drink of tea made with feverfew.

"I doubt he'll take it," I said, and heard the tremor still in my voice. "He fights us."

"Try him," she said.

Mary had by now got Nat covered up in the bed. I gave her the cup, and she lifted his head and shoulders and tried to persuade him to sip. He took a little.

"Sit with him awhile," she said, "and I'll clean myself. I stink of prison." And she added, seeing my look of fear, "Would thou rather I asked Hester?"

"No!" I said. I wouldn't let her think me a coward. So I sat and watched, and from time to time I bathed his forehead with cool water and helped him to drink. He was hot and glassy-eyed but no longer raving. When Mary reappeared in clean clothes, I left her with him and took the dirty linen downstairs.

Hester was still at work in the kitchen.

"Thou should go now," I said. "Don't risk contagion."

"I will, shortly."

She was bruising some leaves in a mortar.

"What's that?" I asked.

"Feverfew and sage, and some pepper. It's to lay on him when he's quiet, before the fit comes again. Fetch me some soot from the fireplace. It must be fine and powdery."

"How much?"

She passed me a small spoon. "To fill this."

I scooped up the soot, and she tipped it into the mixture; then she separated an egg and dropped in some of the white, stirring it all together.

"Thou'll need some strips of cloth," she said, "to bind it in place. Tell thy mistress to lay this on his wrist and it should ease the fever. I'll go back to the Mintons' now and not return. I won't risk infecting the children."

"I'm afraid Deb'll fret for me," I said, "but I can't have her brought here, into a house of sickness."

"I'll take care of her, the poppet. I like having a little one around."

"Deb's no poppet," I warned, but she laughed and went out.

After a while Nat's fit passed, and he lapsed into calmer sleep. Mary laid on the poultice, and we both waited on God in silence.

Later, when we were downstairs, eating a bite of supper, she said, "Well, thou seest how all my principles come to naught?"

I didn't understand, and said so.

"Most Friends won't leave prison," she said, "even to die. I thought to be the same. But when the boy fell sick . . . I could not let him die there, in that foul place. And I could not let anyone else care for him. So I have paid the fines, his and mine. But others will do their three months."

I thought of Abigail Minton, crying to her mother to let the fines be paid. Who was right? Mary or Elinor?

"I would do the same," I said, "for someone I loved."

She was silent awhile. Then she said, "I never had a child. Other women seemed to have them — and lose them — so easily. I believe that God gave me my barrenness so that I could use it in his service — preaching, and printing. . . . Well, I have bought my time, and must use it. I'll start the works up again; print some pamphlets. Thou can help me, if thou hast a mind to."

"Oh, yes! I've done some printing with Nat. And I still practice writing — and reading." I thought of the poems of George Herbert and how I'd wanted to talk to her about them.

"We will print, then, when this crisis is past. And, God willing, Nat will recover."

Next morning Hester came to the back door with news from the prison. Her eyes were brimming with tears. "Hannah Davies is dead — and her so young and leaving a child not five months old. Last night we lost our friends Edward Beale and Luke Evans. And others falling sick all the time. No one wants to be in court today — judges, jury, or ushers. They're saying it's a black assize and will spread sickness through the town."

I thought of Will, and my fears for him returned. Would he be in court again?

"There's my mistress sick with the fever," Hester went on, "and now my master has it, too; and our neighbors willing to pay the fines, but they won't have it. I've said to my mistress: Think of thy children. She says the Lord's will is clear to her, but it seems to me if the Lord gives you children, you should care for them. And with the weather so hot, and the overcrowding, it breeds sickness. . . ."

When I went up later to the sickroom, Mary was sitting beside Nat with her eyes closed. I thought at first they were both asleep, but Mary opened her eyes and said, "Has Hester gone?"

"Yes."

"Thank the Lord. She runs on so, and her voice carries through the floor."

"She's been kind," I said, "and helped me with the work."

She gave a weary smile. "Oh, I know, she's a good soul. But I never could abide her endless chatter."

That night Nat's fever rose again. The rash was bright red now. He tossed and turned, only half-conscious, and felt burning hot. Mary refused to leave his side. She did not cry or say she wished things had been otherwise, but occupied herself bathing his forehead or encouraging him to drink sips of the herbal tea. Often she simply sat in silence with her eyes closed.

I cleaned and tidied the kitchen, then took down Mary's Bible and sat reading by candlelight until my eyes grew tired. The house was quiet; I missed Nat's teasing and laughter. Alone, by the embers of the fire, I prayed for his recovery.

With jail fever in the house, I would not go to the conduit in the morning, but Em, who had heard of our trouble, took my pails and fetched water for me.

"They're saying in town that the Quakers will spread sickness," she said.

"Only because they are so crowded in prison!"

She ignored my logic, and glanced at our house with a disapproving look that seemed to include my mistress, the sick man, and the entire business.

"You'd be best out of this, Su. Find another employer. The tailors would have you; they're looking for a girl."

"I would not desert Mary!"

But she was no longer listening. Something had caught her eye. "Here comes your young man," she said.

"Will!"

I darted outside, causing Em to step back.

He was down the street, heading my way. The joy of seeing him overcame my fear.

"I'll leave you two together," said Em, with a knowing smile. She lifted her yoke.

"I thank thee, Em." I said it absently, all my attention on Will, who had seen me and was hurrying toward me.

"I *told* thee not to come!"

"I had to. How is Nat?"

"Sleeping now; the fever comes and goes. He's —" My voice broke and I choked back sudden tears that were perhaps as much to do with Will as with Nat. "He's in God's hands."

"I had to see thee. We've not spoken since first-day." He reached out to me, but I stepped back over the doorstep. "No! Don't touch me. I may carry the fever on my clothes."

"If there's danger, I'll share it with thee."

"No!" He seemed to me reckless, childish even. "Folk are dying, Will. If thou should die, can't thou see it would break my heart? Thy father's, too. He must love thee, in spite of all."

"Susanna! Let me come in! I've told my father I mean to marry thee. I'll leave home, find work. We'll be together, man and wife — if thou'll have me?"

211

His eyes searched my face, warm and eager. I felt such a rush of longing for him that it was all I could do not to run into his arms.

"Yes," I said. "Oh, yes! I'll marry thee — if God wills it." He let out a breath and stepped forward — and at once I put my arms out, straight and stiff, to keep him off. "But stay back now! Be safe."

"Susanna." He was smiling. "I'll come tomorrow. No, don't argue. I'll come. Here on thy doorstep. Every day until I can hold thee again. And I'll pray for Nat. For all of you. I love thee, Su."

"I love thee," I said. "Now go." And I closed the door.

Without stopping to pick up the pails of water, I ran along the passage, upstairs, and into the room I shared with Mary. I opened the window wide and leaned out and watched him walking away up the street, hidden for a moment behind the jettied story of the next house, then in view again, his tall figure moving quickly between groups of maidservants and carts and early-morning traders, until I could see no farther, and he was gone.

I drew the window back, and sat down on my bed.

Married. We would be married! I wanted to tell the world, to share my joy. But I could not leave the house, and Mary was sleeping, exhausted, in a chair by Nat's bed. And perhaps, I thought, as soberness returned, the news should wait. Everything must wait until Nat was well and the house clear of sickness. I could hold my secret until then.

Susanna Heywood. William and Susanna Heywood. The names had a good sound.

William

I walked home as jaunty as if I had won a prize. The day seemed to sparkle, and I smiled at everyone I met. It was only later, when I reached home, that I realized what a long way I still was from achieving that independence I had promised Susanna.

My father kept me busy in the shop and warehouse all week. The court sessions had finished after two days, and the justices went home — thankful, no doubt, to be away from the risk of jail fever. Several prisoners had collapsed in court, and the lawyers and councilors had sat through the proceedings with posies of herbs at hand. A woman outside the courthouse had done a brisk trade selling them.

True to my word, I went every morning to see Susanna. Nat's fever raged all week, but on sixth-day

Susanna told me, "He's weak, his heartbeat faint. But the fever is going down."

"God be thanked." But I had heard that people who survived the fever sometimes died soon after from weakness or from inflammation of the lungs. I knew Nat was not out of danger. And neither was Susanna. I feared for her in that house of sickness.

I visited the Mintons several times. Susanna had asked me to check on Deb, and I found the child much indulged by Hester and Abigail, and was able to make Susanna happy with news of her.

But there was no news of Judith or her parents, since no one was allowed to visit any of the prisons while the sickness continued. Meanwhile, Sam Minton's business was suffering.

"Judith and our mother did most of the glove-stitching," Tom told me. "With them in prison, and our father, too, there is only the apprentice and me to cut out, and Abby to stitch."

"And I'm not near as neat and quick as Judith," said Abigail.

I thought of the loss of trade and goodwill, and the fines, which might amount to a month's pay for a working man.

"At least *we* are a family business," said Tom. "Isaac's father works alone, and now there is nothing coming in, except what Susanna can earn. And there's the rent to pay if they are to keep their home."

"I shall look for work," said Isaac.

But he was only a lad, not above twelve. He couldn't earn much. I thought of the apprenticeship I had been offered. What wouldn't any of these children give for such a chance? But the answer came: not their souls. They would refuse it, as I intended to do. Their parents had already given up much more.

"Well, the Quaker meetings will founder," my father said with satisfaction as we entered the warehouse on seventh-day. "No one will dare gather, with sickness in the town."

"We *will* gather," I said. "The children will meet as usual." I spoke confidently, though I guessed he was right and we would be a small group and no trouble to the authorities.

"*You* will not go."

"I will. I must."

I was conscious that here, in the warehouse, was the heart of my father's life. All around us bales of wool were stacked, tangible evidence of his wealth and status. These bales would cushion me, if I let them; they would provide the eight hundred pounds for my bond, set me up in a wealthy trade, form my inheritance in due course.

"I saw Nick Barron yesterday," he said. "I told him you accepted his offer."

"What?" Shock and outrage took the breath from me for an instant. "But — but I don't. . . . I am writing . . ." I pictured the crumpled attempts flung into the fireplace, the difficult letter still unwritten. "Thou had no right!"

He ignored this; ignored, too, my use of "thou," which usually provoked him to anger. "You will thank me in due time. Barron was much pleased, he said, and will proceed with the paperwork."

"I cannot be taken on against my will!"

My father seemed unaware of the enormity of what he had done. "You will have a month to see how you like the work," he said, "as is usual. I don't doubt you will fall into the way of it very well. And the sooner it's settled, the better."

"Father," I said. My breath came fast. "Thou cannot direct my life. I will choose my own master. And my own religion."

We heard a door open elsewhere in the building, and voices. Richard and the other men were arriving for work.

My father put a hand on my shoulder. "A month in London, and you'll find you see things quite differently. New interests, new company, all the life of the city. You'll shake off these ideas. And the girl . . .

I know how it is when passion strikes. You can think of nothing else; you must have her. But it will pass, believe me. In London, you'll forget her."

And he drew me away to join the others, quite unaware of my feelings.

I shall refuse to sign, I thought. No: I could not allow matters to reach that point before protesting; it would embarrass everyone. I must write, explain. But to write that letter, now, would be harder than ever, and speed was necessary. I'll tell him, I decided, face to face.

A chance came during the day, when I was sent out on an errand. Nicholas Barron's house is on St. Peter's Street — Peter's Street, as the Quakers call it — a substantial house, much like our own, and no doubt with a family like ours who concern themselves with dowries and inheritances, and who dress in fine clothes and dance and sing and play music, and don't worry too much about religion. An excellent connection, as my father had said, and one I would have welcomed only a few months ago.

A maid answered my knock and went to find her master. I waited in the hall, which was oak-paneled and smelled of beeswax and lavender. There was a lion-legged chair, polished to a dark sheen. The maid had asked me to sit, but I was too nervous.

Nicholas Barron came smiling, though with an air of busyness. "Will! Your father has told me . . ." And, to the maid: "Bess! Fetch some beer."

"No!" I said. "I won't delay thee. My father acted without my knowledge — or consent." I saw his face change. "I am sorry, sir." The formal "sir" came out without my thinking.

"You do not agree to the bond?"

"I cannot make the promise thou ask for, and I will not enter into a bond I may feel obliged to break."

"I'm sorry," he said. "Sorry to lose you. And yet I confess I was in a way disappointed when your father spoke to me. I thought he had persuaded you, that you had conformed. And I was surprised at that. What will you do?"

His abrupt question took me by surprise. "I — I don't know. Leave home. Find work."

"In London, where the streets are paved with gold?"

"Perhaps." I felt I was being mocked.

"You know, without an apprenticeship, you will find it difficult to get work — except of a menial kind."

"I have friends who may help."

"Dissenter friends?"

"Yes."

He gave a little shake of his head. "There is something joyless, humorless, about those people. Don't become like them. Be merry!"

I smiled. "I will try."

"Your father is angry, no doubt, and disappointed. Well, I shall tell him he should be proud to have a son who stands by his beliefs."

"Thank you."

He turned to go, then stopped and said, "If you should find yourself in London and in need . . . my business is at New Bear Quay, near the Custom House. Remember."

And he left me.

I did not tell my father that day about my conversation with Nicholas Barron. My father had not, after all, troubled to tell me of *his* negotiations on my behalf, so why should I do him the courtesy? So I reasoned. The truth was, I feared his anger.

But the next day — first-day — I was forced to tell him.

I arrived home at noon to find my stepmother and Anne back from church and settled in the drawing room, sewing. Their faces told me I was in trouble. When my father appeared, my stepmother rose to leave and took Anne with her. My sister left unwillingly, with a backward glance of sympathy at me.

"You have been to the Quaker meeting, I suppose?" my father began.

"Yes."

"Do you intend to get yourself arrested even before the bond is signed?"

"There will be no bond," I said. And I told him what I had done.

He stared, and I saw amazement in his eyes. He had not believed I could refuse such an offer.

"You turned it down? It is settled?"

"Yes. All is clear now."

He rallied then, and his bullying manner returned. "And how do you intend to live?"

"I shall find work."

"What work? You have no trade. Your dissenting friends are all shoemakers and tailors and the like. They work with their hands. They have skills. Society needs them — for their work, at least. You are fit for nothing but idleness."

"Thou speak as if I wasted a fortune on gaming and drink!"

"I'd rather you did! Rather than this — this overthrowing of all religion and respect. It would be easier to understand. . . ." He paused, and stared. "What's that mess on your coat?"

"Horse turds. Some boys set upon us."

He made a sound of disgust. Nothing distressed him like damage to good cloth. He turned to me, almost pleading. "You'll end in prison. And you don't understand what it's like: the filth, the cruelty. People *die* in prison, Will. They die of fever, of poisoned air and water, from being fettered and beaten. More die in prison, I'd guess, than are ever strung up for public execution. They'll throw you in with the very dregs of society: thieves, whores, pimps — murderers, even. How do you think I'd feel if you were rotting in some jail? Or sent on a prison ship to Jamaica? If you won't care for yourself, think what it would do to your sister, to your stepmother, to know you were in such straits."

"I know it will hurt thee —" I began, but got no further, for he exploded in sudden fury.

"Do not 'thee' and 'thou' me! I will not endure it!"

"A generation or so back, everyone spoke like this," I said.

"But they don't now. Now it is damnably rude, a sign of an upstart who will not defer to his betters. You will find no work if you 'thee' and 'thou' people, unless it be with the dissenting sort." He paced the room in exasperation. "I had looked to see you apprenticed, then setting up in your own business, successful. Married, in due course . . ."

I said, unwisely — but he made me unwise — "I *will* marry. With Susanna."

His face darkened. "That —"

"Don't call her any foul name," I warned. "I won't hear it."

"I will call her no right wife for you! What are her people? Village artisans? A weaver, you said?"

"Yes, and not to be despised. There would be no cloth merchants without weavers."

"I don't despise them. They have their place in society. As we have ours. But how could I call such a man kinsman? How could you bring a girl like that here, to this house, to be sister to Anne? You'd do the lass no favor. She would be lost, out of her place."

I remembered the night of the midsummer dinner, how I had thought: Anne would love this, but I could not imagine Susanna here at all. He was right. I belonged here, but Susanna did not. So my future must lie elsewhere.

Susanna

*T*here came a day — more than a week after Nat had left prison — when we knew he would live. The fever had passed, the rash was gone, and the demons no longer tormented him. Although weak and exhausted, he took food, and by the evening insisted on leaving his bed. He came down to sit by the kitchen fire — for he felt the cold, even though it was summer — and talked, and played with the cats, and even joked with us as he used to.

Mary, who's not one to fuss, fussed. She sent me upstairs for a warmer coat; she made a posset, and stoked up the fire instead of letting it die down as we usually did of an evening.

Later, when Nat was gone back up to bed — breathless on the stairs, but steady — we both gave thanks to God. Mary sat in silence for a long time with her eyes closed, and I did not disturb her.

Next day we swept and fumigated, opened the curtains, threw out dusty herbs, and brought in fresh ones to sweeten the air.

Mary opened up the shop and print room and sent me to Castle Street to ask Simon Race to come to work. She'd been writing a pamphlet about the trial and the conditions in prison and planned to get it printed and on the streets.

I came back along High Street, called on the Mintons, and gave them our news.

"God be thanked!" said Hester, and she scooped me up into a great hug. She knew the danger we had been in. "Thou'll be staying there now, with thy mistress back, but the little one" — she nodded at Deb, who was riding past on a hobbyhorse in pursuit of Joe, and hadn't even noticed me — "she can stay as long as she likes. Isaac, too."

I could not call on Will, though I passed his father's house. But when I returned to the print works, Mary said, "Will was here."

"Oh! I missed him?"

She saw my dismay and smiled in sympathy, and for a moment I thought she, too, would hug me; but she only patted my arm. "I told him to come this evening," she said.

William

I went straight to the printer's that evening, telling Joan not to hold back supper for me. Mary was shutting up shop when I arrived. She led me through to the living quarters at the back, where Susanna was stirring a pot on the fire and Nat was seated nearby with a cat on his lap.

"Nat!" I said. "I thank God to see thee recovered!"

In truth he looked so wan and thin that I was shocked. His cheeks were pale, and his eyes seemed to have sunk. If the fever could do this to a young healthy man, I thought, no wonder that people were dying.

I turned to Susanna, and she looked up, rosy-faced from the fire.

"Susanna."

I longed to hold her, to tell her how much I'd missed her, and I saw the same longing in her eyes.

"Sit down, Will," Mary said. "Thou'll stay for supper?"

"Yes. I thank thee." I sat on the bench next to Nat, and we all exchanged news. Mary was concerned at my decision not to go with Nicholas Barron. "That was a hard choice for thee," she said, "and distressing for thy father, who thought to do well by thee."

"But I feel I was right."

"This Nicholas Barron sounds a good man," said Susanna, "and understanding."

"He is. But my father . . ." I sighed.

"Thou should honor thy father," said Mary.

"I do. Truly. And I love him. There used to be so much love between us. But now he will not listen to me."

"It can break hearts," said Mary, "when families are split. And our people are often blamed for it."

"Is there news of Friends in prison?" I asked.

"Yes. We heard last night from the Stonegate. The fever is gone from there. Judith is well. Dan Kite has been beaten, but both grow strong in the spirit. At the Castlegate there is still much sickness and no one can visit."

She handed me a piece of paper with wording for a pamphlet on it, written in black ink. "What dost thou think? Susanna and Nat approve."

"Concerning the PERSECUTION OF THE INNOCENT PEOPLE OF GOD CALLED QUAKERS," it began, and went on to describe the attacks on the meetings, the beatings and unjust imprisonment, the overcrowding in the jails.

"It is all true," I said.

"Simon has set the text up ready. Tomorrow I must try to find a man to operate the press. John is still in prison and determined to suffer for the truth."

"I could do it!" I said. Here, at last, seemed an opportunity. I could work in Mary's print room.

But Mary looked at me and shook her head, smiling. "I mean a man, not a youth. A big man, strong. The press requires it. I thought to hire someone from Bridewell: a vagrant, perhaps."

I felt rebuffed. First my father, now Mary, thought me unemployable. "Let me try, at least," I said.

"Try now," she said, and opened the print-room door.

The press dominated the room. The huge screw at its working center was operated by pulling a lever. I'd seen John haul on this, using both hands.

Mary brought the tray of type set up by Simon and placed it ready. "First we must ink the type." She indicated the daubers and poured ink onto a flat plate.

I inked the daubers. These were not so much

228

heavy as difficult to manage. With one in each hand I dabbed awkwardly and was slow.

"Thou need set up a rhythm," said Mary. And she took them from me and daubed quickly, her wrists surprisingly strong — right-left, right-left — till the type was covered in ink.

"Then the paper goes here, and is held under the frisket." She slid it into place and turned the handle that moved the bed of the press into position. "Now try the bar."

I used both hands and pulled. It was heavy, but the screw turned and the weight came down.

When we moved the bed back, Mary pulled out the result: a perfect page.

"Concerning the PERSECUTION . . ." It looked at once more impressive in print.

"Well? I did it!"

"Then do another."

We printed another page, and a third. Nat came in from the kitchen to watch.

By the fifteenth page I was tired, and by the twentieth my neck and shoulders ached and the strain must have shown in my face.

"Could thou run off sixty?" Mary asked, a glint of laughter in her eyes. "A hundred? Five hundred?"

I smiled and shook my head. "Find thyself a vagrant."

Nat came to my defense. "He'd build up strength in no time. And the daubing: practice is all it needs."

I looked at the tray of print, set in mirror image so that it must be read from right to left and with the letters facing backward. It looked like some strange foreign script. There were large initial letters to be incorporated, too, and spacer blocks. And all must be checked for errors.

"To learn all these tasks would be useful," I said.

Mary looked at the two of us in amusement.

"Dost thou seek to be my new apprentice, Will? Nat will be leaving me soon."

I turned to Nat. "To London?"

"Yes. I've been given names — Friends, printers — who will help me find work. I want to be away before summer's end."

Mary cuffed him lightly on the cheek. "He'll walk to London that can scarce walk upstairs without puffing! But we'll get thee well, boy. Come and eat."

After supper Nat went to bed, being still tired from his illness. Mary then found something in the print room to busy her. I knew she was giving me time with Susanna.

We came together, arms tight around each other.

"I've missed thee," she said. "It's been so long — more than a week!"

"Shall I give thee a kiss for each day?"

"One for each hour!"

We laughed at first, and then our kisses grew more eager.

"We won't be separated again," I promised. "We shall marry." I took her by the hands. "Tell me how Friends marry. There is no priest, so how is it done?"

"We — the couple must bring their wish to be married to the meeting. . . ."

"And?"

"And declare, each in turn, that they will take the other. Each one promises to be — with God's help — a loving and faithful partner until death shall separate them. And so the meeting is witness."

"No one marries them? No elder? No justice of the peace?"

"It is the work of the Lord."

"Then no one can stop us? We can be wed?"

"If it be God's will. Yes."

Mary rattled the door of the print room before she opened it. When she came in, we were standing hand in hand and something of our intent must have shown in our faces, for she looked at us sharply and said, "What's afoot?"

Susanna said, "Will and I wish to be married."

She stared. "Married?"

"Soon," I said.

Mary looked from me to Susanna and back to me. "Susanna is my servant," she said, "and has agreed to stay with me for one year. She is but fifteen years old. And thy age, William?"

"Seventeen."

"And thou hast offended thy father, and turned down an apprenticeship, and must find work?"

"Yes."

"In Hemsbury?"

"I think it's best to leave Hemsbury." I glanced sidelong at Susanna. We had not talked about this.

"Because of the quarrel. Yes, I see that. So thou'll leave Hemsbury. And go where? And do what?"

"I — don't know. Perhaps London. Perhaps book-selling. Or printing. London is where most chances are, I believe."

"And while thou travel and seek work, and probably do not find it since thou hast had no apprenticeship, and must take to the road again; while thou hast no home and no money, thou'll take with thee a young wife, who will soon be swelling with thy child — no, don't blush, these matters must be faced. Would thou have thy wife give birth in a barn? Or a ditch?"

I felt humiliated, and tears stung my eyes. I could

not look at Susanna. I said in a low, choked voice, "So thou'rt against me, like my father? I thought to have help from thee." And I knew I sounded childish and gave fuel to her argument.

Mary said, more gently, "It's a fine thing for young men to be on the road, making their way. Not so easy for a woman."

Susanna gripped my hand. "I'm not afraid," she said. "I love Will, and if he goes to London I'll go with him."

"Thou'rt not free to go. I forbid it."

"Then we'll stay here," I said, "for a year. I'd work for thee, Mary, willingly — learn the printing trade." Even as I said it, I knew it was not what I wanted. I felt my life narrowing.

Mary looked at me, and it was as if she saw my thoughts. "Under thy father's eye? No, Will. Thou hast given up much for thy faith. Don't give up freedom. Marriage is for settled men who can offer a home and a steady income. Perhaps one day thou and Susanna will be wed. But not now."

"If we could ask the meeting —" Susanna began.

"The meeting is largely in prison."

"But we may have enough present for witnesses."

"Witnesses must be of full age, and willing. I for one am not willing."

Mary put a hand on Susanna's shoulder. "Hast thou spoken to thy parents of this?"

"No. It came about" — she looked up at me — "only this week. But I fear they will think like thee." Her fingers curled tight around mine.

Everyone is against us, I thought. But there must be a way.

Susanna

$\mathcal{M}$ary hired a man from Bridewell. A strong man, he was, a laborer with a thirst to match his strength. He'd been locked up for brawling in the street. He called us "you quaking folk" and was glad of the work.

We printed a hundred sheets quarto, and priced them at a penny each. I helped fold and cut. All the time I was thinking not of our meeting and its troubles, but of Will and whether he would go to London, and how I might manage to go with him, and whether we'd find Friends in London to be witnesses to our marriage. I could not bear the thought of him going without me.

On seventh-day we were out with our pamphlets. It was market day, the streets full of traders' booths, and to swell the crowds further there was a sheep fair in the Abbey Fields and a hanging on the edge of town. We stayed away from the hanging — of a woman who had beaten her servant girl to death — but we heard the roar of the crowd as the ladder was kicked away; and then saw, some ten minutes later, the movement of people returning from the spectacle, lit up and talking of it.

Mary and I stood on a mounting block in the marketplace and cried our wares, and a little way off were Will and Tom, also selling pamphlets. Nat, who was still frail, minded the shop. The children were about town. I suspected they had sneaked to the hanging; such things fascinate Isaac, and no doubt Joe is the same.

My brother and sister had stayed on at the Mintons'. Hester loved having Deb there, and I knew Mary did not like small children overmuch, so it suited us all.

I was surprised how many people stopped and bought pamphlets from us.

"Those pamphlets will be kept," said Mary, "and read and reread; and read aloud to those who cannot read; and so the truth is spread."

But we were not long allowed to spread the truth. A group of men began shouting at us. One snatched up a pamphlet, tore it, and threw it in my face. We heard a man shouting at Tom and Will, wagging his finger at them, threatening the stocks first, then purgatory. A crowd gathered, and soon constables appeared, armed with clubs. Their leader demanded a copy of the pamphlet and declared it unlicensed and illegal. They hauled us down, and I saw Will and Tom manhandled and their pamphlets taken. The crowd grew excited. The hanging had inflamed them, I think, and they craved more. A cry went up: "The stocks! The stocks!"

I panicked at that: pictured the stocks; imagined being forced to sit there in the filth of the marketplace with my legs through the holes, my skirts bunched up above the knee, and folk gaping. The thought terrified me.

The constables rounded us up, the two of us and Will and Tom.

We were lucky. It seemed the stocks were full. Some pickpockets had not long been penned there, and an idiot boy who raved and cursed, spittle running down his chin. So we were warned and sent on our way and our pamphlets confiscated.

"We'll go back to the shop," Mary said.

But it was my free time now, after noon.

"I must find Deb," I said.

And I wanted to stay out with Will. Mary knew that.

She gave me a sharp look. "Mind thou'rt back in good time. And take care that thy conduct is seemly."

I felt hurt. She was unfair. I was never late back, and my conduct was always — nearly always — seemly. It's because of Will, I thought; she wants to keep us apart.

Mary went off, and I joined Will and Tom. They both looked pleased with themselves; the scuffle seemed to have enlivened them.

"We had some interesting talk," Will said, "with a Baptist, and then others who go to church but favor freedom of worship —"

"And others who just wanted a fight!" said Tom, and they laughed.

We were free now to move among the stalls. No one recognized us.

"Does thy father know thou'rt here?" I asked Will.

"I told him I was going to the market."

"He won't come for thee?" I was afraid of Will's father, especially now that he knew I meant to marry his son.

"No. He has customers."

We found Deb with Abigail at a stall that sold sweetmeats.

"We went to the hanging," said Abigail. Her eyes were big. "The woman kicked and choked for a long time. The boys have gone off somewhere. Can I buy Deb a candied apple?"

"Yes. I'll pay. For thee, too." I reached through the slit in my skirt for my pocket. "What's the price?"

The stallholder, a mean-faced woman with dirty fingernails, picked up the sweetmeats that Abigail and Deb chose and wrapped them in a twist of paper. "A penny each," she said.

It was too much.

"I'll give thee a penny for the two," I said.

"Quaker, aren't you? I thought you people never haggled."

"We won't be cheated, either. A halfpenny each?"

She scowled and took the money.

The girls wandered off.

"Take care!" I called after them.

I felt the market was an evil place, full of cheating and false dealing. Mary sold always at a fixed price, as did Sam Minton, and folk came to trust them, and their trade was steady. Here, we must be ever watchful.

"Shall *we* eat?" said Will. "I'm hungry."

From another stall we bought beef pies cooked with nutmeg, cinnamon, and herbs. We walked about, eating and looking at the stalls, and I felt happy just to be outside with Will, to be near him and yet part of a group, so that no one could call my behavior unseemly.

We had wandered to the edge of the market area and were heading down toward the river, when we heard a surge of loud voices. It came from a makeshift arena a little way off, on some rough ground near the river.

"Looks like a cockfight," said Will, and he began to turn away.

But then Tom said, "There's Joe! And Isaac!"

The two boys were at the back of the crowd, trying to see. Their heads bobbed up and down — one brown, one fair.

Tom said, "Joe knows not to gamble or go to such places! Our father would be angry!" He ran, and Will and I followed.

"Joe!" shouted Tom.

His brother looked around, saw him, and squirmed farther into the crowd. Tom tried to push in after him, but was forced back with punches and foul language from those who had placed bets and were trying to watch.

From between the heads of the bidders I saw the small stage below, where cocks were being fitted with spurs and tossed into the ring. Several fled and had to be caught and thrust in again before they would fight. I felt pity for them, even though they were only fowl. Feathers and blood began to fly, spattering the nearest spectators. Combs were torn, crops slit. The damage caused by the spurs was quick and terrible.

"Isaac," I said, catching my brother by the arm. "Thou should not have brought Joe here."

"We didn't bet — only watched."

Isaac is always like this, seeking and questioning. It makes my mother angry, but my father says the light in Isaac is strong and we need not fear for him.

Tom had hauled Joe out and was scolding him. A roar from the crowd signaled the end of the cock-fight. People began moving and flowed past and around us, talking, arguing about the merits of one cock over another.

I don't know why they noticed us, why the mood changed. Perhaps Tom had jostled someone. Perhaps we were recognized from earlier, when we'd been selling pamphlets. Perhaps they just heard our Quaker speech and thought we'd be an easy target. Whatever the cause, we found ourselves surrounded by a group of four or five jeering, drunken youths.

"Quakers! Holy Joes! Come to preach damnation, have you?"

They shoved Tom and grabbed his hat and trampled it underfoot, and when Will went to help him, they set about the two of them, pushing and threatening, then moving in fast with fists and boots. Isaac and Joe rushed to help; I ran and tried to hold them back, and screamed as I saw Will knocked down and kicked. He curled up to protect himself, and I thought: They will kill him, and terror seized me. I turned to passersby, clutching at them. "Help us! Please!"

And then, all at once, it was over. Others — perhaps the cockfight organizers, not wanting trouble — dragged the attackers away. Will got to his knees. There was blood all over his face, and as he dabbed at it, his shirtsleeves and coat were stained red. I dropped down beside him and we put our arms around each other, there in the street, not caring who saw. Out of the corner of my eye I saw Isaac watching this, too, with his usual intent interest.

I knew Will must be hurt, his ribs and shoulders bruised, if nothing more. I could feel him trembling. I drew back and saw that he had a split lip; it was swelling fast, but most of the blood on his face came from a cut above the right eye. I took off my wide linen collar and used it to staunch the flow. The others clustered around. Tom's nose was bleeding, and he was shaken but seemed otherwise unhurt.

Will looked at me and tried to smile. "I'm no street fighter."

"Nor would I have thee be one," I said.

We stood up together.

Joe had found the hats. Will's had a footprint on the brim, and the gray plume was broken and dangling; Tom's was crushed beyond repair.

We were shaken, all five of us. Joe was struggling not to cry, and Isaac came and leaned against me and I put my arm around him.

The area of the cockfight was deserted now except for a few men dismantling the arena. I saw the bodies of dead cocks tossed aside: a little heap of blood-stained remains.

We stayed close together as we walked back into town. People stared, and I was conscious of my bare neck and Will's blood on my bodice.

We went to the print works. It was not until I saw Mary and told her what had happened that I began to cry. But Mary took it all in her stride: fetched water and a wash ball and cloths; sent the boys to fetch beer and food; found a clean shirt of Nat's for Will and a collar for me.

"You were lucky they did not draw their knives," she said.

I shivered, feeling the hostility of the town. And I thought: Tomorrow is first-day. They know where we meet. They will attack us again.

William

I managed to avoid my father that night. I ate with the servants and went straight to bed, and it was not until the morning that he caught me on my way out to Meeting and saw the injuries to my face. I told him it was nothing but a marketplace brawl, but still he was shocked. My coat was bloodstained and my hat damaged, and for once I sensed some relief in him when I refused to accompany him to church.

So I went to Meeting. It was held in the yard of the Seven Stars because the room was locked. I met Mary and Susanna there, but not Nat, who had been persuaded to rest at home. The Mintons came, and Isaac Thorn, and perhaps six or seven other children. The numbers had dwindled with the fever and the sheer hardship of enduring so much for so long.

As we had feared, a mob gathered, and I recognized among the ringleaders the faces of yesterday's gang. With God's help and Mary's guidance we remained still and silent, standing in the cobbled yard while they pelted us with dung and other filth. When Sheriff Danson arrived with soldiers, the crowd dispersed, and it was we who were rounded up, accused of causing a breach of the peace, and driven off with threats and blows.

In the afternoon we returned to find the yard gate closed and a bar nailed across it. We tried to meet in the street outside, but the mob came again, followed by Danson and his men. I began to suspect collusion between them; certainly it would suit the authorities to have a breach of the peace occur, for then an innocent meeting could be declared illegal. This time they arrested Mary and sent her to Bridewell overnight. And they warned the rest of us to stay away.

"This group of Dissenters is to be broken up," said Danson. "The town does not want it. The authorities do not want it." And he ignored me but singled out Susanna in a way that made me fearful for her and suspicious that my father was involved. "You, girl: have a care. I warn you: if you bring these children here again you will regret it. I will make an example of you."

Afterward, Susanna and I went back to join Nat at the printer's. We took Isaac and Deb with us; they were to stay the night with Susanna, since Mary was in Bridewell. Isaac, mighty pleased with himself, told us he had found work: George Woodall, the tailor next door to the Mintons', had taken him on as a servant and errand boy. "Now I can pay Tom for our keep — mine and Deb's," he said.

We gathered on benches in Mary's kitchen and sat in silence; and with a pot simmering on the fire and Deb whispering to her doll, we held the meeting we had not been able to hold at the Seven Stars. The silence grew, and with it my courage. I knew that whatever the authorities planned, they would not overcome us; that the way of compromise and comfort was not the true life, the life of the spirit in which we must be answerable for all our actions. And I resolved to be faithful to that life.

Afterward, Nat allowed Isaac into the shop to browse among the books, while Deb played with the cats and her doll and chattered to Susanna.

Nat asked me how things stood now between my father and me.

"Difficult," I said. "I need to leave home, to find work. We can never agree, and it puts me in the wrong to be living in his house."

"But thou'rt not idle. He has thy labor."

"But does not need it. And . . . it hurts me to see him so disappointed in me — because there is nothing I can do."

The little striped cat sprang onto Nat's knee. He teased it, trapping its front paws in his hands, letting it struggle free before he caught it again.

"Thou could come with me," he said.

"To London?"

I saw Susanna tense and look up.

"Mary has given me names of Friends in London," said Nat. "Printers and others. There's plenty of work there in the book trade."

I had a sense of a way opening, my life expanding. And yet . . . "I might be a burden to thee," I said, "being younger and unskilled."

"Thou'rt a burden I could carry." Nat smiled. "I'd not ask thee, else. London's far off. Truth is, I'd like a friend and fellow countryman with me."

I did not look at Susanna, but I knew her eyes were on me. I heard Deb trying to regain her sister's attention. "Su, look at Sibley. She can ride on puss. Look, Su."

Nat stood up. "Come into the bookshop. I'll show thee."

I followed him out.

Isaac was there, sitting cross-legged on the floor. He had a book of anatomy open on his knees at an alarming picture of a child in the womb.

Nat went straight to the shelf he wanted and took down a book he'd obviously often looked at. In it was a map of London. There was the river, the Thames, snaking between a mass of buildings: blocks and blocks of densely packed narrow houses, and scattered among them steeples and towers, parks, palaces, windmills, taverns.

Isaac put down the anatomy book and came to join us.

"See, here is Paul's steeple-house," said Nat, pointing to the cathedral. "And all around are printers' and stationers' and bookshops. . . ."

I saw a web of narrow streets, and not far away the river with ships clustered on it. "Dost thou have a place to go?"

"No. But I have contacts. There are many of our people in London, many more than here. We would have help and places to stay while we looked for work." He smiled. "What say thou?"

"I'd like to travel with thee. And the book trade: yes, that, too; it would interest me. When will thou go?"

"Not till summer's end. No hurry yet. Thou'll need to resolve matters with thy father, I know."

And with Susanna, I thought. But I did not mention her, being unsure what to say, or even what I wanted. Nat had offered me friendship, help, company on the road; but could that include Susanna?

When I left, after supper, Susanna came to the door with me. Deb, who had resisted all attempts to send her to bed, clung to her sister's hand, still chattering.

Susanna's eyes were somber. "Thou'll go to London, I suppose, with Nat?"

"I'd like to," I said. And added impulsively — for surely Nat would not mind? — "Thou could come, too." I knew Quaker women traveled, sometimes alone, to preach and visit friends in prison. It would be impossible for a girl like my sister, but perhaps not for Susanna?

"I am promised to Mary for a year."

"A servant's bond can be broken. It happens all the time." And yet I knew I would not want to do it myself.

"I gave my word," she said. "And besides" — she looked at me straight, unblushing — "I can't take to the road with two young men."

"If we could be married —"

I went to put my arms around her, but she stepped back, glancing at the child, whose eyes flicked from one to another of us.

"We can't talk now."

"I'll find a way," I promised. "I won't desert thee."

But her face was downcast. When we said good night she kissed me briefly, as friends do in greeting, and I knew it was not only the presence of Deb that held her back; my enthusiastic response to Nat's suggestion had hurt her.

I walked home, feeling stirred and unhappy. I meant to go straight to my room to think, but my father appeared as soon as I opened the hall door.

"Where have you been all day?"

I took a breath and answered, "Waiting on the Lord."

"Waiting on that whore!"

My fists clenched. But he was my father; I must give him respect. "Don't call her that."

"What else can I call a girl who walks about the streets with men? A girl who stands up on a mounting block and shouts her opinions to the marketplace, and distributes this — this package of filth and lies." He thrust one of our pamphlets at me. "And you — consorting with her openly. I heard all about it after church. People were eager to tell us: how they had seen Alderman Heywood's son yesterday, walking through the town with blood on his face, and a brazen slut hanging on his arm."

"It was not—" I began, and stopped in exasperation. What point was there in trying to explain?

"You shame me, and endanger my position in the town," he went on. "You shame my wife and your sister—"

"How?" I cried. "How can what I do shame any of you?"

"Because we are your family! You reflect on us. You are part of us."

"Then I will sunder from you!" I said, and saw him recoil in shock. "I will give up my family" — I heard my voice break — "and if they wish it, I'll never see them again. But I will not give up my faith and I will not give up Susanna."

"Will . . ." He stepped forward, hands extended. "Will, you're young. You see everything in black and white. You know, many people have doubts about religion, or ideas that don't suit. Your own mother: I know she worshiped in secret. And no harm done. As for the girl, if you want her, take her. No harm there, either. But don't think to marry her. You must come to live in the world as it is."

"I won't live in your world," I said. "It disgusts me. There must be a better way to live."

And I bade him good night and went up to my room.

There, I paced up and down the short space

between door and window, going over all the conflict of the day. I could break with my family, go to London with Nat; but I saw no way that Susanna, being so young and bound to Mary, could travel with us — or any way that we could be married.

I heard the family come upstairs to bed, voices on the landing, doors closing. When all was quiet, I slipped out of my room and went down to the kitchen to get a drink.

Joan was there, scouring the cutlery ready for morning.

"Oh, Master Will!" she exclaimed. "You'll be wanting beer? And something to eat? There's venison pasty left over from dinner. . . ."

"No, Joan. I've eaten. A mug of beer will be enough."

She poured it for me, regarding me critically as she set it down. "You look a ruffian with that cut on your face!" Joan had been with us since I was eight years old and spoke to me sometimes as if I were still a child. "And what's that shirt you're wearing?" She looked closer. "Poor, coarse stitching on it."

"It's a friend's."

"One of those Quakers?"

"Yes."

"I saw you in the marketplace on Saturday with your Quaker girl. Pretty lass. Oh, come, Master

Will, you don't look very cheerful tonight! What's amiss? Some new trouble with your father? I heard the two of you shouting."

She sat down opposite me, broad and motherly, her eyes sympathetic.

I sighed and put my head in my hands.

"I want to marry Susanna," I said, "but my father will not have it. Well, thou'll know that already; this house must shake with our quarrels. But the Quakers will not agree, either; and Susanna's parents don't know yet but are sure to say she's too young. Everyone is against us. And I don't know what to do."

Joan regarded me shrewdly. "Folks can always make a vow of marriage between them if they want to," she said. "They need only find witnesses."

I ran a hand through my hair. "I know. But I don't want that sort of marriage. It doesn't seem right and proper. And my father would probably declare it void."

Joan nodded in agreement. "I have heard," she said, "that there's a priest on Hog Lane, on the edge of town, who performs marriages out of church. Quick and secret. No banns."

I looked up. "A priest?"

She nodded. "Anglican."

"But . . . is it legal? Would we be properly wed?"

"Oh, you'd be wed safe enough, before witnesses.

And you'd have your certificate." She looked at me anxiously, as if half regretting what she'd said. "If you're sure that's what you want? It's a big step, to break with your family. The master's a hot-tempered man. He'd be furious; might disinherit you. And what would your girl bring?"

"Nothing. I don't care about that!"

"You can't live on love, Master Will."

"Then I'll work. What would the license cost?"

"A few shillings more than usual, you can be sure."

"I have a little money . . . Hog Lane? Near the Stonegate? What's his name? When could I see him?"

"I don't know, sir. But I'll find out for you."

"Soon?"

"Soon as I can. Leave it with me."

She got up and began putting away the knives and spoons, the sand box and the cleaning cloths. "Take your beer up to bed with you, sir. It's time I snuffed this candle."

Susanna

I was eager to see Will the next day, but in the afternoon Tom came with a message that he was gone with his father on business to Ludlow and would be away all week.

All week! And we had parted last night with a sense of misunderstanding. I had been longing to see him again, to make everything right between us. Now the week stretched before me, empty; I could not reach him and didn't know what he was thinking about me, what changes of heart he might have had. I felt abandoned, angry with Nat, angry with Henry Heywood for taking Will away from me, and angry with Will for being so quick to obey his father.

Mary soon noticed my mood and guessed the cause of it.

"Will does right to obey his father in every way he can," she said. "It is his duty. And thine is to obey me. So get that yoke over thy shoulders and fetch some clean water. And when thou hast done that, there's the meat to be bought for the men's dinner, and the passage to be swept . . ."

"I *know*," I said sulkily.

"And don't use that manner with me! Keep busy," she added, more kindly, "and the week will fly by. Nat and I plan to get another pamphlet on the streets. Thou can help, if thou'rt willing?"

I bit my lip and nodded. "Yes. I am."

Later that day, she came to me with an idea.

"Thou hast time owing to thee," she said, "and Friends say there is no fever at Norton jail. Why not go there one day and visit thy parents?"

"Oh, yes!"

I felt a mixture of pleasure and guilt — guilt because I had pushed my parents to the back of my mind. I'd been unable to visit them when Nat was ill with the fever and there was a fear of contagion, but now I remembered that they had been several weeks in prison and I'd given little thought to their suffering; they must long to hear news of Isaac and Deb. And I would tell them about Will, and how much I loved him. Perhaps they would disagree with Mary and allow us to marry.

When I thought of this, I wanted to go straight-away, but the weather was thundery most of the week, with great bursts of rain that bounced off the cobbles and sent everyone scurrying for doorways and overhangs. I went to see Judith in the Stonegate prison instead. In the end it was sixth-day before I left for Norton.

It's a day's walk there and back, so I rose at dawn. I took some bread and cheese, tied in a cloth, and a flask of beer, and a straw hat of Mary's to keep off the sun, and set off early.

I remember little of the journey there. I reached Norton and found my parents well, though greatly crowded in prison, and my father in pain from his joints. I told them Isaac had found work and that Deb was with Hester, who thought her a poppet. They were glad to see me looking well.

When I spoke of Will, and our wish to be married, they said I was too young and must be patient, that Will must make his way in the world, that if we truly loved each other we would wait — all such talk as I did not want to hear. And I saw that they would neither challenge Mary nor give their consent. But I could not plead with them in that place, surrounded by other people.

And so we parted, and I set off home. The day was warmer now, and I was tired and walked more slowly. In the fields on either side of the road, rows of men and women were at work, hoeing around onions and turnips, or harvesting cabbages. Sometimes I'd see one stand and arch backward to ease stiffness. Children crouched, pulling weeds with quick, small hands. I remembered, in lean years when my father was in prison, working alongside my mother in just such fields, hour after hour. A day's work is long in summertime.

I met a few people on the road: farmers, mostly, or women coming home from market. I was perhaps halfway to Hemsbury when I saw coming toward me on foot a man in a white shirt and a high-crowned black hat — a man whose very walk I knew and loved. . . .

"Susanna!" he shouted, and people in the field nearby looked up. He ran toward me, and I ran, too, and he caught me in his arms and swung me off my feet.

I squealed and fell laughing against him. There was no one to see us, only the field workers, who didn't know us and didn't care. All the gloom of the last week lifted from me in a moment. We stood with our arms around each other and I breathed in the smell of him, warm from the sun, and felt his heart beating.

"When did thou get back?" I spoke into his shirt and had to look up and repeat the question.

"Yesterday. Late. And then today I had news to tell thee, and hurried to the shop, and found thee gone."

"What news?"

He looked down at me, his face bright with his discovery. "I have found a way for us to be married."

I felt a surge of hope, of delight. In an instant I saw the London project dropped, the two of us staying together. "How? Has Mary changed her mind?"

"No. It is a priest. I went to see him this morning —"

"A *priest*?" I let go of him and took a step back. "We'd be married in a *steeple-house*?"

"Not in a steeple-house." He caught my hands. "A room in an inn — or anywhere else we wish. But he'll marry us without banns. No one need know till it's done. He could marry us on Mon— second-day."

"A priest?" I said again. A shadow seemed to have fallen on the day. "I thought — I thought always, as a child, that one day I'd be married in Meeting, before God, and with my friends as witnesses. Not . . ."

"It's not what I would wish, either," said Will, and I saw that the joy of his news had gone out of him, and was sorry. "But God would be there, within us. God is always there. And it *is* marriage, legal and binding, and not to be challenged. And afterward, we can come before God in our own way, and no harm done."

"But this secrecy," I said, and began to walk slowly along the road. "I don't like it. We should act openly, in the truth."

"It's not right, I know." His face was eager. "But, Susanna, think: once we're married we are free to do as we will! Thou could come to London with me and none to hinder it. Or stay here, and I'd come for thee when thy service was up. No matter what happens we'd be man and wife, and that bond would be stronger than any other, even parent or master. It's a small wrong, but the end is the same."

His eyes sought mine, pleading.

It did not seem a small wrong to me — marriage performed by a hireling priest who would come between us and God.

"He will not read the Anglican marriage service if we don't want it," Will said. "Only what's necessary to make it legal. He is accommodating."

Accommodating. The word did not reassure me.

"Marriage is a holy thing—" I began.

"And dost thou think it would not be holy between us, whatever the means?" He caught hold of me and began to kiss me. "I love thee, Su."

I kissed him back, but I felt low in spirit; something had been spoiled. He sensed my lack of response, and after a while he let me go and we walked on in silence, no longer touching. My eyes filled with tears, which I dashed away with my hand. Will walked a little ahead of me, looking at the ground. I was forced to scamper to keep up with him.

"Art thou angry with me?" I asked.

"No."

"Thou *seemst* angry."

For answer he put an arm around my waist and pulled me close. It was uncomfortable walking like that, but I preferred it to our former separateness. Now and again I glanced at his face. It was shut to me, the eyes downcast. I knew I had hurt him.

I thought: He will go to London soon. And I looked back toward Norton, southeastward. It had taken me half a day to reach Norton; another half-day would have brought me only as far as Brentbridge. I tried to imagine the great distance between this home country of ours and the capital. Hundreds of miles — hundreds of miles of fields and woods and winding roads and villages and hamlets and towns and great cities like Oxford. He will go to London, I thought, and I will never see him again. He'll be caught up in his new life, make new friends, perhaps meet another girl; and he'll forget me. If I don't marry him now, I'll lose him.

And I thought: After all, he's right; what does a ceremony matter? It's the intent behind it that counts. We can go through with it, and afterward we can make all well again before God and our families and friends. But at least the thing will be done and no one will be able to part us.

"Will?" I said. My voice came out small. "I have decided. I will marry thee."

He looked at me and gave a little shake of his head. "I don't want to force thee."

"Thou dost not. It was a shock — no more. Thou'rt right. It's the only way. Let's be wed — on second-day, as thou said."

"Perhaps we should consider longer."

"No." I was anxious now, afraid to delay. "On second-day, in the evening, when I finish work." I put my arms around him. "Unless thou hast changed thy mind?"

"No," he said. "I have not."

We walked on, hand in hand. There were grassy banks on either side of the road, stretches of woodland, hedgerows full of flowers. I remembered my daydream of the field at Long Aston. We were promised to each other now, and had we been in merrier mood we might have stopped and taken advantage of the freedom we had out of doors and felt no shame in it. But our near quarrel had subdued our spirits, and besides, the sun was low in the sky and Mary would be expecting me. We reached the walls of Hemsbury, and dropped hands as we went through the gate and into the town.

One thing came to my mind. Where would we go, on second-day, after we were married? Not to Mary's house or Will's father's.

I was too shy to ask him. But wherever we went, I thought, if I did not return soon after, I'd be missed, and explanations must be made. And when I thought of those explanations, I had a sense of unease.

William

I knew as early as seventh-day morning that something was afoot. My father seemed unusually anxious that I should not go to Meeting the next day. Of late he had become resigned to my absence from church and had not tried so hard to prevent me leaving the house on first-days. But now he said, "You'll come to church tomorrow, Will. I insist on it. To see you knocked about and bleeding as you were last week—"

"That did not happen at the meeting," I said.

He frowned at the interruption. "We worry about your safety. There may be trouble tomorrow. You could be injured, or arrested."

I was at once alert. "Is trouble planned? Father? What dost thou know?"

"Do not 'thou' me!" he exclaimed, and he used this as an excuse to lecture me and avoid answering my question.

I could gain no more from him, and wondered whether I should warn my friends; and yet they would come to Meeting whether or not they were warned, and what could I tell them?

In the afternoon I visited the priest and arranged that Susanna and I would meet him at the White Hart on Hog Lane at six o'clock on second-day evening. We were committed now, and I entered a state of agitation that took everything else out of my mind. After the ceremony Susanna would be my wife. We would be left alone together in the room at the inn, free to love each other. That was something that, when I imagined it, made me feel both eager and nervous. But there was guilt, too, and unease, caused by Susanna's misgivings and the secrecy of it all. I tried not to think of the time when we must confess what we had done.

That night I lay awake for hours, and it seemed I had no sooner fallen asleep than I was woken by birdsong and saw that it was almost dawn.

At once a thousand thoughts flew into my mind. Since there was no chance of more sleep, I decided to leave the house before my father woke and tried to prevent me. I rose quietly and washed in last night's cold water, dressed, and crept downstairs and out the back way.

I went straight to the printer's, where Nat, yawning, answered my knock. Susanna was in the kitchen, making up the fire. I kneeled beside her and spoke quietly, telling her what I had arranged with the priest.

"Oh, Will!" She turned to me, and I saw in her face the same mixture of emotions that I was feeling. We were like two conspirators, and I jumped up as Mary came in.

"Thou'rt early, Will," she said.

"Yes." I told her about my fears that trouble was planned.

"If there is trouble, the Lord will prevail," said Mary. She measured oats into an iron pot. "Porridge? Thou'll eat with us, I hope?"

"Yes, I thank thee."

While the porridge cooked, we sat in silence. Mary gave the pot an occasional stir, and Susanna poured beer and passed mugs around, but we did not talk more than was necessary, each of us mentally preparing ourselves for whatever was to come.

It came sooner than we had expected. We had eaten and were about to leave for Meeting when we heard a banging on the shop door. We all tensed and glanced at each other.

"Wait here." Mary went through the print room and into the shop, and I heard her open the door; then came a man's voice, and the sound of people entering, the scrape of boots and clink of weapons.

Nat hurried after Mary, but in a moment he was back. "The sheriff's men," he whispered. "They've come to question us and seize copies of the new pamphlet."

"On first-day?" exclaimed Susanna.

"It's a ploy, I reckon, to prevent us being at Meeting. Go out through the yard. Thou too, Will. There's a way along the backs of the houses."

"But—" I began. I did not want to run and hide if Mary was accused.

"Thou can't help here. I'll stay. Go quickly, before they stop thee."

So we left, Susanna and I, out past the cesspits and middens of the backyards and into a side alley; and from there we ran to Cross Street.

The children were already there, and I caught Tom's look of relief when he saw us. The gates to the Seven Stars's yard were still barred, and the children stood in a small but defiant group in the street outside.

We drew together, joining hands for support.

Almost at once a group of youths appeared — the same ones who had attacked us the week before.

They began tormenting us, and soon after came the sheriff, with several constables.

The sheriff's men moved in fast, striking out with their clubs. This time there was no attempt to declare our meeting illegal or to protect us from the youths, who disappeared. The aim was to break up the meeting with violence. The constables forced their way in among us and laid about them with their clubs, striking even the little ones. I caught Susanna to my side and tried to shield her from the blows. The younger children were screaming. I saw Tom struck as he went to protect his sister, Joe and Isaac beaten back against the gates.

Susanna had been standing her ground, but when she saw Isaac attacked, she broke from me and ran forward. A constable caught her and threw her down hard on the cobbles. As he went to strike her, I flung myself between them — giving her time to scramble to her feet. The blow landed on my back, and a kick brought me to my knees. Two men seized me and hauled me upright, and I saw Susanna also held, and heard Sheriff Danson shouting that we were all under arrest.

He turned on Susanna. "I warned you not to bring these children here again!"

"I brought no one." She was breathless from her fall, but defiant. "They came of their own free will to worship God."

"You are the ringleader — and you'll suffer for it."

I protested at the unfairness of this. "We have no leader! I am as much to blame as her."

Danson turned to me, and a look of irritation crossed his face. "Master Heywood."

I was breathing hard and could feel blood trickling from my nose. "Do not ask me to go home," I said. "I will not. You must arrest me, too. This is an outrage against innocent people, against children —"

"Take them all to Bridewell!" said Danson.

They took even the youngest ones. I could not reach Susanna, but saw her ahead of me, pushed and harried by the constables. No one struggled, and no one showed tears. They took us through back alleys — I think to avoid townsfolk who might be moved to sympathy. Some who did see us cried shame on our guards, but in general people were at church or within doors and the streets were empty.

I saw now that the authorities thought to have broken the meeting once and for all. The youths had given them their excuse to label us riotous and disorderly; the raid on the print works — unheard of on the Lord's day — had prevented Mary from being here, Mary being the person they found most formidable and difficult to deal with. What was left, they thought, was a clutch of children who could be terrified into submission with beatings and imprisonment.

I had never been inside the Bridewell before. The yard, which contained a stocks and whipping post, was awash with filth: rotting food and the contents of a blocked and overflowing cesspit. As the soldiers handed us over to our jailers, I managed to reach Susanna and take her hand. We all tramped through the filth of the yard, watched by the inmates.

Two ragged women cackled at sight of us.

"Here come the Quakers!"

One of them, with a nod toward me, called out to Susanna, "Does he keep his hat on in bed?"

Susanna ignored them and kept hold of my hand. I tried not to let my disgust at our situation show in my face, but I must have failed.

"It's not so bad here," she said. "Not as bad as the Castlegate. And we will probably be out in the morning."

I felt ashamed. "I should be comforting *thee*."

"No. It's new to thee."

"I'm glad I am here."

And I meant it. At last I had forced them to stop treating me like an alderman's son.

Once inside, we were separated and saw no more of each other. Susanna and the younger children were put to work picking oakum, but Tom and I were sent to join a group of men who were breaking up stones. It was heavy work, and we soon tired, but if

270

we stopped, the overseer beat us. We were fed twice that day on gruel and coarse bread, and given a ration of beer. As I worked, I thought: I must learn to endure this; it could be far, far worse. And I remembered how Daniel Kite had been manacled and chained for weeks in a damp, stinking hole.

The day was hard, the night foul with coughings and pukings, moldy straw and the squeaking of rats. Tom and I huddled together. I thought I'd never sleep, such was my fear and revulsion, but I dozed an hour or so before dawn and woke, stiff, to harsh voices calling us to work.

We were not let out till noon. I caught occasional glimpses of the children, but did not see Susanna and had no chance to seek her out. Then, as the inmates were shuffling off to line up for their bread and beer, we found we were free to go. The jailer jerked a thumb at Tom and me. "You two: out! You're released."

We stumbled into the yard. I ached all over from the stone-breaking. The children were assembling there, along with other people who were to be released. I looked around for Susanna — at first casually, expecting to see her, then with increasing concern. I scanned the crowd, the yard, the entrances to workrooms. My heart began to beat faster. Susanna was not there.

I found Abigail. "Abby! Where is Susanna?"

"Oh, Will!" She turned a stricken face to me. "The sheriff's men came in the morning and took her away. They said she was to be put in the stocks."

"The stocks?" I looked around wildly. The stocks were empty.

"Not here," said Abigail. "The public stocks. In the marketplace. They say she is our leader and a trouble-maker and must be punished."

Susanna

They didn't tell me till the morning what was to happen. The first I knew was when the constables summoned me. When I was told that I was to suffer three hours in the stocks, I heard my voice rise in a wail as I cried out, "Why? What have I done?"

The constable in charge held an official-looking paper. "You are charged with holding an illegal meeting and with encouraging and leading others into defiance of the law."

The children pressed forward to support me.

"You must take us all!" said Abigail — and I loved her for that, for I knew she was not brave by nature. A clamor of voices broke out, the children protesting, the jailers forcing them back as the two constables seized me, one holding each arm, and marched me out.

Isaac broke free and ran after us. "Take me instead!"

The jailers dragged him back, and he called out, "Su, don't fear, we will come and stand beside thee!"

But the constable in charge told me, "Your friends are to remain here till noon."

I looked around, desperate, for Will, but he was nowhere to be seen. I was set apart, alone, and thought I would faint from fear. The stocks are the punishment I have always most dreaded — more than beating or even prison. To be shamed in public, jeered at, pelted with rubbish. . . . I shan't be able to bear it, I thought. I'm not like my parents, not like Mary; my faith is not strong enough. And I began to sob as they led me away.

Before, when I had been marched through the streets, it had been with friends. We had walked together boldly, proudly, and let the taunts pass over us. This time it was different. I saw people stop and stare, a child point and look up to question his mother. And I knew how thieves and whores and other outcasts must feel as they are dragged to punishment, alone and friendless.

The market was busy when we arrived: maids and housewives out with their baskets; awnings flapping in the breeze; stalls laden with bread, fish, cabbages, onions. We moved through it all and came to the open space where the stocks stood. There were three sets, all empty; so I was to be alone.

They took me to an end set, unlocked the bars, pushed me down on the cobbles.

"I will sit," I said, struggling to regain some dignity. "You need not force me."

And I sat and put my legs obediently into the two curved spaces. Even so, they manhandled me, one of them putting his hands on my legs and pushing up my skirts so that my calves and the tops of my stockings were exposed, before bringing down the bar and locking it. My arms were put into the top section and that, too, was locked in place. Then, as if attention enough had not been drawn to me, one of them shouted a proclamation of my crime so that all knew of it. And then they left me there, a prisoner.

I had stopped crying. The tears were all inside me, but I knew I must not show them. I was a witness for the truth and would have them think I suffered gladly. All around, people had heard the proclamation, and faces turned to look: curious, mostly; some cruel, some sympathetic, but many indifferent — for after all this was nothing much as far as they were concerned, a minor punishment, something to be seen every day. I tried to look back at them without flinching.

I thought of Will, of how we had planned to be

married this evening. And I thought: He will be released at noon, and come straight here, and see me like this; and the thought was unbearable.

At first no one threw anything. Then some children appeared, little grinning boys of seven or eight. They didn't care who I was or what I'd done. I'd been put there for their amusement, and they soon found the means. A spatter of fishheads came first, smacking into my face and slithering down. Then cabbage leaves, mud, horse dung, which hit me full in the face so that I had to shake my head and blink to see, causing them much merriment. After a while they became a nuisance to traders and were chased away; and a man came and wiped the dung from my face and took the opportunity to slip a hand inside my bodice. Instinctively I moved my right arm, but it was trapped, and he laughed.

I became aware of pain, which grew worse. Under my buttocks the cobbles were hard, and no matter how I shifted about, I could not find ease. My shoulders ached, and there was pain all along the backs of my legs, which were fixed and unable to bend.

But the worst pain was the humiliation. A dog came nosing around, stopped, and urinated against my trapped left leg. Some youths laughed at the sight, and I thought I would die of shame. I knew I must take my attention away from my plight if I was to endure it. I remembered the time when I saw the scars on Mary's back and asked her, "How can thou bear to be shamed like that in public?" And Mary had said, "I wait upon God."

So I closed my eyes and shut out the faces and with it my shame; I tried also to shut out the physical pain. Thoughts crowded in and clamored to be heard: thoughts of Will, of our marriage, of London, of what my parents would say, of what dangers might be to come. But I knew I should not dwell on them now. I let them go. I turned toward the inward light and withdrew into it. A long way off, it seemed, there was mocking laughter. Someone spat in my face; a woman's voice hissed, "You people should be hanged!" I kept my eyes closed and imagined the light expanding within me. And at last I reached a state of peace; I knew that I could overcome all things and that nothing devised by man could hurt or shame me while I was held in the love of God.

Three hours I stayed there. Mostly folk ignored me, though a few could not resist making taunts or throwing rubbish. I tried to remain in that place where such things could not reach me.

It was perhaps two hours into my ordeal that I opened my eyes and saw Mary and Nat making their way toward me through the crowd. They had only just heard that I was there. They came and squatted on either side of me and we endured the mockery and rubbish together.

After a long time Mary's hand touched my cheek. "They come to release thee," she said.

I looked up and saw the constables coming — and then, behind them, Will, pushing through the crowd, his face a mask of distress. He arrived as they began to free me, and Nat hurried to calm and restrain him. The top bar was lifted and my arms freed, and then the lower one. My legs were so stiff I could scarcely move. I got onto my hands and knees and Mary helped me to stand.

Will cried out, "Susanna!" and came toward me, but I shrank from him, unable to bear that he should touch me in my besmirched condition. I hid my face in Mary's shoulder.

Mary began to lead me away. Behind me I heard Will protesting, and Nat urging him to wait. "We'll go to the Mintons', Will, get washed and decent, help the children. . . ." And I heard Isaac's voice, too, and Abigail's.

"Nat will see to them," said Mary. "Let's get thee home; then all will be better."

I nodded, unable to speak. I felt suddenly too weak to do anything for myself.

Back in our kitchen, Mary heated water and found clean clothes for me while I sat by the fire, trembling with shock. The little striped cat jumped on my lap and I stroked it and let its purring comfort me.

When there was enough warm water, Mary filled a tub and put a bag of lavender in to scent it; she brought a wash ball and a jug, and hung a clean linen towel to warm by the fire. She helped me to undress, for I was still shaking and could hardly bear to touch my soiled clothes. Then she went upstairs for her own wash while I took off my shift and stepped into the tub. I crouched and scooped up water with the jug and poured it over my head and washed my hair, rinsing it clean again and again. I washed all over and then sat in the water with my knees bent, releasing the stiffness and letting the scented steam warm me. Gradually I stopped shaking.

When I stepped out, the towel warmed me more, and I rubbed myself briskly and turned a rosy pink. I was sitting in a clean shift, drying my feet, when Mary came down.

"Thank thee for the bath," I said. It was a rare pleasure for me to wash in that way; a bowl on the washstand was all I usually had.

"Did it help thee feel better?"

I managed a smile. "Like a lady."

"Well, be a lady. Thou need not work this afternoon."

"I'll empty this tub!"

"No. I'll do that. Dry thy hair; don't catch cold."

She went into the print room, and I sat by the fire with my head dropped forward and spread out my hair with my fingers, trying to smooth out the many tangles caused by the washing. And all the time I was thinking: about the ordeal I had endured, and the discovery that had come out of it, of the love of God and the power of the spirit. And I thought about Will, and what I must find the strength to do.

A while later I heard voices, and jumped up as I recognized Will's.

Mary came in, shut the door behind her, and said, with a half smile of exasperation, "Will is here and insists on seeing thee! May I send him in?"

"I'm not dressed!"

I was still in my shift, no stays, my hair loose and damp. Mary picked up the clean skirt and I stepped into it; she fastened it while I put on my bodice.

"There! Thou'rt decent enough," she said.

I was still lacing the bodice when he came in.

We ran and clung together without words. I wanted never to let go. With his arms around me, my head against his beating heart, I felt safe. No indignity, no punishment, could hurt me now.

When I looked up, I saw that his face was wet with tears.

"Don't cry," I said. "I'm not hurt. No harm's done."

He dashed a hand across his face. "I should have been there. I should have been with thee."

"But I have survived. See? I am strong." I bit my lip to stop it trembling.

"Oh, Su!"

We kissed, and I tasted tears and did not know if they were mine or his.

"Thou'rt beautiful like this," he said. "Thy hair, thy dress loose . . ."

He kissed my face, and then my neck, and I felt with a small shock of pleasure his warm hands on my breasts, inside my shift. There was a soft, unfolding feeling low in my belly, and as we kissed and pressed against each other, I remembered that this was to have been our wedding day.

"Will . . ." I broke free and took his hand and drew him to sit on the bench beside me. His face was flushed and he looked more desirable than ever before. I put my arms around him and kissed him again, but as we drew apart I told him, "I can't marry thee, Will."

It was said.

He leaned his forehead against mine. "I know."

But did he understand?

"Not today," I said. "Not this year. I don't know when. One day, if God be willing."

He pulled me into his arms and hid his face in my

hair. "I know," he repeated. "I already knew, only I would not attend to the inward light that told me so."

I thought of Mary and our parents, and how we had planned to deceive them all; the priest who would bend the law for payment; and the well-used room at the inn. We were free of all that now.

"Thou'll go to London," I said, "and I shall stay here, with Mary, as I promised. I'm too young to marry, and I have Deb and Isaac to care for, with my parents in prison."

"And I have no money, and no work. But I'll find them. And I'll write, Su — and thou must write to me. I'll stay true to thee. And one day . . ."

"When the time is right," I said, "I'll know. And then I shall come to thee. And no one shall prevent me."

William

I knew I had hurt my father, perhaps beyond forgiveness.

"Who *is* he, this fellow?" he demanded when I told him I was going to London with Nat. "What's his trade?"

"His name is Nathaniel Lacon. He's a journeyman printer."

"And how will the two of you travel?"

"We'll walk. Stay with Friends — other Quakers. Perhaps get work helping with the harvest along the way."

He made a sound of contempt. "You know nothing of the world! You'll have no servants. How do you think you'll manage, on the road, without clean linen every day, with no one to cook your meals or make up a fair bed for you at night?"

"I don't care about those things."

The truth was, the prospect of the journey filled me with a sense of adventure. I imagined sleeping in barns, lighting a fire beside the road at night, bathing in streams.

"You will come to care," my father said, "when you are cold and hungry and the rain soaks your clothes." He turned on me, and spoke bitterly. "I was prepared to spend eight hundred pounds on you, to set you up as an apprentice in the silk trade — and you have thrown it back in my face. You could have gone to London as a merchant, not as a vagrant. Well, you'll get no money from me for this venture. I disown you — cut you off."

For the three weeks or so that followed, until the day I left, we scarcely spoke. It was as if I no longer existed for him. I had one final sitting for my picture in the family portrait. He had always accompanied me before, taking much interest in the likeness, pointing out to Mr. Aylmer details of clothing and background that needed to be included. But this time he would not come, and I went with my stepmother and Anne, who were always eager to see it.

When the session was over, I looked at the almost-finished painting, and saw myself as I should have been: a serious-looking youth standing at his father's side, richly but not showily dressed; dark hair to the shoulders, a collar edged with point lace, one hand holding a book. That was the image of me that would remain with him.

"You have hurt your father greatly," said my stepmother when we left.

"I know, and I'm sorry for it. But there was nothing else I could have done."

She looked at me in astonishment. "You could have obeyed him, done his bidding, as was your duty. Each of us has a place in society and obligations to fulfill. Not all are welcome, but they must be attended to. These people you mix with will destroy all order in society."

But the servants were sympathetic, and so was Anne, who came to me wanting to know where I would stay in London, and when she might come and visit me, and whether I would give Susanna a love token.

"You should give her a ring with both your names on it."

I laughed and shook my head. "Susanna would not wear a ring."

"A lock of your hair, then."

"Maybe. But don't fear. We won't forget each other."

Of the time that was left, I spent as much as possible with Susanna. Mary's kitchen became my second home, and Susanna and I were able to meet most days in the shop or around the workplace. But Mary saw to it that we were rarely alone together for long. I think she had a concern not so much for Susanna's virtue — for she trusted me — but that we should work and learn and become worthy partners for each other; that I should learn the skills and work patterns of an artisan and Susanna those of a woman who can work alongside her husband in his business; and that we should be friends and workmates as well as lovers. "Then you may decide freely, when you are older," she said, "whether or not you will become man and wife." So we both helped in the print room, inking, folding, cutting, and stacking, and served customers in the shop, and took orders for goods.

As the time of departure drew nearer, Nat and I studied maps and planned our journey to London, or looked at the maze of streets that made up the great city. Susanna joined us. I knew she must feel that I stood on the brink of a new life, while she was to be left behind. As for me, I felt as if I were being torn in two.

On our last evening together, we sat on a bench in Mary's backyard, kissing and talking and making promises. The sun went down, and stars appeared, and bats flickered past in the dusk, and still we would not go in, though Susanna shivered with cold. I wrapped my coat around us both and held her close, breathing her breath and feeling her heart beating against mine. We stayed like that until Mary tapped on the door to remind us that decent folks were ready to lock up and go to bed; and then we kissed each other a last good night.

I walked home heavy-hearted, and as I began packing — leaving most of my possessions behind — I thought how much I would miss not only Susanna but the home where I had grown up; and I wondered whether I would ever see my family again.

I planned to take little with me, since I had to carry it all on my back. A change of linen, breeches and stockings, a blanket, a Bible, some money in a pouch hidden under my coat. As I sorted through my clothes, something fell and rattled on the base of the chest. It was a small flute I'd bought in Oxford, years ago. I put it to my lips and played a snatch of a tune.

Many of my new acquaintance would not approve, I knew. I'd heard of a music teacher in London who burned his instruments after he turned Quaker. But I loved to play, and could not believe it to be ungodly. And Nat, I felt sure, would be of the same mind. I put the flute into a bag I could wear at my waist. I'd take it with me. The thought of music on the road was cheering.

❖　❖　❖

The morning dawned fair, and I was up early. The women were still in their rooms, but I had heard my father go downstairs. I carried my pack down, placed it in the hall with my hat on top of it, and went to find him. The door of his private room was half open. I could see him within, standing with his back to me, looking out of the window.

"Father," I said.

He turned around. I stepped into the room and, on an impulse, went down on one knee and bowed my head as I always used to do.

"Forgive me for hurting you, Father. Give me your blessing on my journey."

For a long moment I was conscious of him standing there, the hem of his coat close to my face. Then I felt his hand touch my head.

"Oh, Will . . ." he said, and his voice broke.

I stood up, and we flung our arms around each other.

"What have you done?" he said, his face wet against mine. "You have ruined your life, destroyed my hopes. I *can't* forgive you. Don't ask it."

"Then wish me Godspeed," I said.

"Godspeed . . ." He held me close, then abruptly pushed me from him. "Go," he said. "Get out, before I beat you. And don't write to me from London. I shall not reply."

Susanna

On the morning they left, Mary and I walked with Will and Nat as far as the East Bridge. A light mist was rising from the river, but the day promised fair, and I sensed the excitement in the two of them at the prospect of the road ahead.

Mary was brusque as ever, but I knew she was sad to lose Nat, who had been almost a son to her. I kissed Nat, and then Will. All my goodbyes to Will had been said in private the night before, and now I could only tighten my arms around him and whisper, "God keep thee safe."

"And thee. I'll write — as soon as we arrive."

And then they were on their way, and all that was left was to watch and wave until they reached the bend in the road and were lost to sight.

Mary patted my arm and drew me back toward the

town. "We must comfort each other now," she said.

In the days that followed I felt a great emptiness, and thought I would never be happy again. When I was minding the shop I looked at the maps and tried to work out how long it would be before Will and Nat reached the city, how long before we could expect to hear. All I could think about was the promised letter.

Mary became impatient with me. She took me out of the shop and found housework for me to do: cleaning, shopping, laying the buck-tub on washday. "Work is the way to overcome grief," she said.

And then one day she came to me with a proposal.

"I could do with another hand in the print room," she said, "now that Nat is gone. I would not offer thee an apprenticeship — thou would not want to be bound for seven years — but what say thee to an agreement for a shorter term? If thou stayed with me two years, or three, I might teach thee much of printing practice and bookselling and accounts."

"Oh!" I said. "Yes! Yes, I'd like that."

I saw myself at eighteen, no longer a maidservant but a woman who could read and write, a woman with a trade.

"We could get a girl in to help with the housework perhaps twice a week," Mary said, thinking it through, "but thou must be ready to turn thy hand to whatever's needed in shop or house."

I nodded, willing. Mary's offer was generous, I knew. An assistant who stayed only three years could never repay the time spent teaching her.

"Then let's put it to thy parents," she said.

Now, though still yearning for Will, I began to feel more purposeful. Mary and I visited my parents in prison; an agreement was made and put into writing, and I was able to call myself a printer's assistant. Em was astonished, and saw no advantage for me in the new arrangement, only more work, but Judith understood and approved. Judith was still in prison: thin, with a lingering cough, but calm and determined in spirit. She told me that she and Daniel Kite had promised to marry when they were released; and that when he had enough money saved for their passage, they would sail to America.

The first-day meetings continued, but we began gathering in a Friend's house instead of in the street. The harassment lessened for a while, but Mary warned me that our troubles were not over; already there was talk of harsher penalties. "I believe it will be worse in the years to come," she said. "But with God's help we will endure."

I wondered often about the future, and what it held for me. I thought of Em, with her young man: the comfortable, conforming life she planned to live. I might live like that if I chose. But, despite all danger, I knew I would not. "Stay at home and spin," the vagrant woman had advised me. But that was not a choice; not in these times.

At the end of September the authorities released all the prisoners who had served their sentences. I took Isaac and Deb home to our parents in Long Aston and stayed a few days. We met with Eaton Bellamy Friends, and there was talk of finding an apprenticeship for Isaac. Tom Minton had found a master in Bristol, and would leave home before winter, and Isaac had thoughts of going there, too.

I told my mother about Will, how I missed him and had not yet heard from him.

"Oh, it's hard to wait for news!" she said. "But he is in God's hands. We are all held in the love of God. Have faith."

And at last, one day, the letter came — two letters, in fact, for Mary had one from Nat. Both were brought by a Friend traveling on business.

I held mine, looking at the wax seal, the direction with my name on it, hardly able to believe it was for me. I had never received a letter before.

I took it up to my bed to read; I sat enclosed by the screen, broke the seal, and unfolded it.

He was well. He and Nat were living with a Friend, a printer, in a street near Paul's steeple-house. Nat was employed as a journeyman printer and Will had been taken on as an assistant at a book-seller's. He was happy, he wrote, and had made many new friends at meetings in the city, but no one he loved to be with as much as me. (That line I read again and again.) He told me much more: about the city, the river, the books he sold, the people he met, the meetings they'd had on the way. I read it all, but it was his words of love that I read most eagerly: that he missed me and longed for the time when we could be together again. "Write to me soon," he said.

I wrote the same day. My letter was not as long as his, for I still found writing difficult and must take much care with it. I told him all that had happened here, and ended:

I know nothing of letters, or what is right and proper for a girl to say.

But I will tell thee that I love thee, and miss thee; and when I am free to come to thee I shall leave my home and family and let no one hold me back. When I think of that day, all the long miles that separate us seem as nothing.

I pray God keep thee in the light and watch over thee till we meet again.

Thy friend, Susanna Thorn.

COMING SOON:

Will and Susanna's romance
continues in *Forged in the Fire*

William

*For the hand of Susanna Thorn,
at Mary Faulkner's printing shop in Broad Street,
Hemsbury, in the County of Shropshire.
The third day of June, 1665.
Sweetheart: I write in haste, and in expectation of
being with thee soon after midsummer. I have
money enough saved now, and James Martell will
shortly give me leave of several weeks so that I may
return to Hemsbury and—if thou'rt willing—
bring thee back as my wife. Write to me soon, love,
and tell me that thou agree. Thou know how much
I miss thee. I think of thee every day and long to
hold thee in my arms again. Thy parents, thou
hast said, are willing for us to marry, and if thou*

will speak to them and to the elders, we can be married in Eaton Bellamy Meeting as soon as may be arranged. As for my father, I fear there can be no reconciliation. He has never replied to my letters and I am not of a mind to ask his blessing now.

Make all straight with thy parents and the meeting, love, and with Mary; though I know she will not try to hold thee back. For my part, I cannot leave for a few weeks because my employer is still in poor health. We are both only recently out of prison; the business is in disorder and there is much to be done.

I shall use what free time I have to look for rooms for us, but will put money on nothing until thou hast seen it and agreed. Londoners live crowded together; there are many places to rent but not all are fitting. Nat and I lost our room in Pell Court when we were last in prison, so our address has changed again. We are now at Thomas Corder's, next to the Blue Boar in Creed Lane. The room is not so comfortable as the other, being cramped and ill-lit, but we have few needs and are both saving our wages: I to come to thee and be married, and Nat to set up in business on his own.

Nat will travel with me to Shropshire. He is homesick, I believe, and also wishes to see us married and to see Mary again. We plan to leave on the twenty-sixth of the month, and will travel on horseback with London Friends who are bound for Wales.

The weather here grows hotter by the day. They say there is plague in Holborn and St Giles, but we have none within the city walls. Pray God we shall be spared. Our Friends Robert Osman and Solomon Eccles go about the streets naked, crying repentance, as Dan Kite once did in Hemsbury. There is much talk of the city's evil and of God's wrath; but truly I believe there are many good people here.

I look forward to being outside the city soon, in the clean air of the countryside, coming closer to thee every day. Till then, love, may God keep thee safe.

Thy own,
Will Heywood

Hardcover ISBN 0-7636-3144-2